CLAY BRENTWOOD BOOK THREE: HAMMERSHIELD

D1739364

Creative Texts Publishers products are available at special discounts for bulk purchase for sale promotions, premiums, fund-raising, and educational needs. For details, write Creative Texts Publishers, PO Box 50, Barto, PA 19504, or visit www.creativetexts.com

CLAY BRENTWOOD: BOOK THREE: HAMMERSHIELD
by Jared McVay
Published by Creative Texts Publishers
PO Box 50
Barto, PA 19504
www.creativetexts.com

ISBN: 9781724080929

HAMMERSHIELD

By

JARED MCVAY

An imprint of Creative Texts Publishers, LLC

Barto, PA

This book is dedicated to Jerri Burr, for whom there isn't enough room to say how thankful I am to have her by my side.

"You are my rock…"

Thank you to all my readers. It is true, you're a big part of why I write, and because of your many responses, you're the reason I write what I do.

A writer may think up the stories and put them down on paper… but it's the editors, graphic designers and publishers who turn it into a viable product.

To those people, I say, "thank you."

PROLOGUE

-

Clay Brentwood was exceptionally fast with a six-shooter, and uncommonly good with a rifle, along with the fact that he could hold his own in a knock-down-drag-out fistfight; a reputation he never wanted and hoped to one day live down.

Deep down, he was a rancher who wanted nothing more than to raise horses and cattle and come home to spend his evenings with a wife and hopefully, children.

But his life was turned upside down when Curly Beeler and his gang raided their ranch and raped his pregnant wife, Martha, killing her and their unborn child.

Over Martha's grave, Clay vowed Curly and his gang would be held accountable for the atrocities they'd committed.

Two and a half years later, Clay finally caught up with Curly and his gang in a small town down in New Mexico territory.

After avenging his wife's death, Clay was ready to lay his guns down and go back to being a rancher, but fate had other ideas.

Bill McDaniel, head of the Texas Rangers, arrested him for the murder of the man who'd raped and murdered his wife.

After being sentenced to hang by a misguided judge, McDaniel got the case retried by a different judge, and now three and a half years since it all began, instead of being hung as an outlaw, Clay had been sentenced to serve two years as a Texas Ranger, under the guidance of the legendary Bill McDaniel.

An outlaw by the name of Aaron Hammershield, an outlaw Clay knew to be a killer, was to be his first case.

CHAPTER ONE

-

Around six in the morning, a cold wind with gale like force came roaring out of the north, driving its way down the main street of Austin, Texas. Giant tumbleweeds rolled down the street, bunching up in front of doorways, making them impassable. By ten o'clock in the morning, Austin looked like a ghost town.

Clay Brentwood stepped out of the hotel and was almost knocked off his feet by a gust of frigid air. Turning up the collar on his sheep lined coat, and pushing his hat down on his head, he headed down the sidewalk in the direction of the Texas Ranger's office. He'd only been a ranger for a few days and already he'd been the target of a would-be gun slick who was trying to make a reputation for himself. Young hotheads these days, seemed to think being fast with a gun and killing a man made them big.

Clay Brentwood was a man who went out of his way to avoid trouble, but somehow, trouble seemed to track him down and push at him until he had no choice but fight.

He was about to make his way past the saloon when the doors came flying open and two drunken cowboys charged into the street, cussing a blue streak. Squaring off, they pulled iron and commenced emptying their pistols in the general direction of each other. They were both drunk and wobbling around so badly in the heavy wind, lead was flying in all directions.

A bullet ripped a tear in the front of Clay's coat, just about chest high, and a second bullet put a hole in the brim of his hat before he could find a post to hide behind.

Angry, Clay ran into the street. Something needed to be done before somebody got killed. Holding his pistol by the barrel, he clubbed the first drunk he came to on the top of his head. The man dropped to the street and lay there.

Turning toward the second man, Clay saw he was already lying flat on his back. He wasn't sure what put him there, the rotgut he'd been drinking, the heavy wind, a bullet, or maybe a combination of all three, but he wasn't taking any chances and put his foot down against the man's wrist before reaching down and taking the pistol from his hand.

Shaking his head, Clay realized there had been no real danger, the man's pistol was empty and he could see no blood. The man had passed out and was in no condition to hurt anyone. He knew this because the man's loud snoring could be heard over the raging wind.

Clay was staring down at the two drunken men lyin' in the street, wonderin' if he should drag the bodies onto the sidewalk before a wagon or some horses came through when the city marshal ran up. "What's all the shooting about? What's going on here?" he asked, not noticing the Ranger badge pinned to Clay's coat.

Pointing at the two men, Clay said, "Two drunks were trying ta kill each other. This one's passed out from too much who shot John, and the other I knocked on the head with the butt of my pistol."

"Now see here, you have no authority to…." he said, then noticed the star pinned to Clay's coat. "I'm sorry, ranger. I… I didn't realize..."

Clay looked at the marshal and shook his head. The man was dressed in an eastern style suit, a derby hat and wore high top shoes. There was no gun hanging on his hip, nor was there a bulge where one might be hidden inside his coat. He had pale skin and only stood just a little over five feet tall. In Clay's opinion, the man was a dude and was about as qualified to be city marshal as a ten-year-old girl – maybe not even that much.

"You need ta keep ah tighter rein on this town, Marshal," Clay said with a sneer. "Ah person could get shot just walkin' down the street, mindin' his own business."

The would-be marshal glared at him and said, "You rangers think you're so tough, well let me tell you…"

Without a word, Clay leaned into the wind and continued on down the street, leaving the marshal standing there, talking to himself.

The marshal's eyes followed Clay for a moment, then shifted to the two drunks. Being a city marshal had seemed exciting at first, and his brother-in-law, the mayor, had said it would be an easy job; but after three months in this hellish town filled with drunken cowboys, fist fights, shootouts, and the ladies society league on his back every day, he was ready to show the city of Austin, his overbearing wife, and the state of Texas, his backside. He was more than ready to go back to Vermont where a man could live among decent, civilized folks. Yes, that's exactly what he would do, just as soon as he could find someone to help get these two drunks out of the street.

-

Clay Brentwood walked into the Texas Ranger's office and headed straight for the coffee pot. He could do with a cup of coffee; especially on a day like today. The coffee was hot, black, and strong. Unbuttoning his coat, Clay ambled over and sat down on a high-backed chair in front of the ranger's desk.

Bill McDaniel looked up, nodded, and then went back to what he was doing.

"You really gonna make me do this?" Clay asked, sipping on the coffee.

-

Bill McDaniel, head of the Texas Rangers, was a long drink of water with a thick, bushy mustache, and graying hair. It had been said by folks that he had eyes that could see through walls, which of course wasn't true, but he did have an uncanny intuition about people and situations. He had the reputation of never going after a man he didn't bring in, one way or another. And, as the head of the rangers, he tried to instill that same way of thinking in the men under him.

Not only did the men in his command hold him in the highest regard, but if the truth be known, intimidated them more than they would admit.

For the past two days, Bill McDaniel had been doing his least favorite thing in the whole world - paperwork. He'd eaten little, his eyes were red, his back hurt, his clothes were wrinkled, he was bone weary tired, and not in the best of moods.

He looked up and said, "You didn't lose your hearing, did you?"

"No, I can hear fine," Clay said with a puzzled look on his face.

"Well, what about your mind, you get hit on the head and lose your memory?" he asked.

"No, I ain't lost my memory, either," Clay said with a bit of irritation in his voice.

"Then I reckon you remember hearin' the judge say he was givin' you to me for the next two years?"

Clay let out a sigh and said, "Yes, I remember, but…"

"No buts about it," McDaniel said, interrupting, before Clay could say more. "You're mine for the next two years, plain and simple. During that time, you'll be a duly sworn in Texas Ranger, doin' what rangers do best, bringin' in criminals. I'm not only short of men, but you're the only one I can send that actually knows Hammershield by sight, and maybe understands his way of thinkin'."

"But…"

McDaniel held up his hand. "I know you think the judge should have just dropped the charges against you, and well, frankly, so do I. But he didn't and you have to admit, his alternative decision is a bunch better than a neck stretchin'."

"What about bein' shot in the back by some owlhoot on the prod, or facin' down some hot-headed kid who's tryin' ta build a reputation? Dead is dead, ain't it?"

"Still better than hangin', as far as I'm concerned," McDaniel said with a grin.

Clay stared at Bill McDaniel. This was not an argument he stood a chance of winning, and he knew it.

McDaniel stood up and rubbed his back, then said, "But I'll tell you what I will do… you bring in Aaron Hammershield and I'll consider talkin' to the judge about reducin' your time."

A wide grin spread across Clay's face. This was the best news he'd heard in months. Seemed to Clay all he'd done for the past three and a half years was to track down bad men, and in the process, men had died by his hand.

"Any idea where to start lookin'?" Clay asked. "You can bet when he broke out of jail, he didn't hang around Austin any longer than it took him and his bunch ta hightail it out of town."

Bill McDaniel picked up a sheet of paper from his desk and handed it to Clay. "Got a telegram just this mornin'. The marshal up in Dallas believes Hammershield's men robbed a bank up there, and you can bet Hammershield was somewhere nearby to collect his share."

"Dallas? That's over two hundred miles from here. By the time I get up there, they could be long gone," Clay said, exasperated.

"Then I guess you'd better get ah move on. And if he is gone, all you have to do is pick up his trail and start after him before it gets cold," McDaniel said. "Now get out of here. I don't want to see you again until your man is behind bars here in Austin. And I don't care if you bring him back, sittin' upright, or belly down across the saddle; makes no difference to me." As an afterthought, McDaniel said, "If you can figure a way to get a few of the scum that ride for him, well… I'll make sure there's paper on them, too."

"What about expenses?" Clay asked.

"Get receipts and the state of Texas will reimburse you when you get back. But no fancy hotels, women, or liquor."

Outside, the wind was still howling something fierce. Clay was convinced life was not somethin' a man could figure out too easy.

His first assignment as a Texas Ranger, was to go after an outlaw by the name of Aaron Hammershield, and to bring him back one way or another. The problem was, the man was not only smart in the educated sense, but he was also a conniving, ruthless, piece of trash who just plain got a perverse satisfaction outta killin'.

Clay looked up the street toward the livery stable and shook his head. After McDaniel arrested him, thinkin' he might go to prison, he'd left his black stallion with his good friend and neighbor, Marion Sooner, so now he had no horse with which to go Dallas.

Instead of heading for the livery stable, something held him in the doorway. He wasn't looking forward to the long ride.

After a moment, he looked toward the train station and his eyes lit up. If he had to travel, why not travel in comfort? He could go by train! He would get to Dallas much quicker than on horseback. These new trains could travel at speeds up to twenty-five miles an hour. Twenty-five miles was a full day's ride in weather like this. Dallas by horseback meant several long days in the saddle, with beans and bacon for a diet and camp coffee when, and if, he could find water and wood for a fire.

His decision made, Clay turned and headed for the train station. With his head down against the blistering wind, he didn't notice the man in the derby hat standing across the street.

At a safe distance, the man walked down the opposite side of the street and followed Clay to the train station, then stood nearby with his back turned, while Clay purchased his ticket.

The man behind the counter said, "Train for Dallas should be here in about two hours, or so, if it's on time. That would make it about six o'clock this evening. With the other stops the train has to make, should put you in Dallas somewhere around seven o'clock or so, tomorrow morning. Would you be wanting a sleeping berth?"

"How much extra will that be?" Clay asked, reaching into his pocket.

"One dollar," the ticket taker said.

Clay laid the money on the counter as the man wrote out his ticket.

"You'll be boarding just in time for supper. Have a good trip, Ranger."

Clay looked at the station attendant; curious at how he knew he was a ranger? He hadn't said anything.

The station man grinned and indicated the badge on his coat.

Clay grinned and said, "Oh yeah. Thanks."

After Clay had gone, the man who had followed him into the station walked up to the window and also bought a ticket to Dallas, but not one with a sleeping berth. He didn't plan to be on the train long enough to need one. He would be off and gone, long before it reached Dallas.

Tyrone Brewster walked out of the station; confident this was going to be an easy job.

At five foot eight, average build, brown eyes, brown hair, brown suit, derby hat, and no scars or distinguishing marks, he looked just like any other drummer riding the train. Only, he was no drummer. He was a bringer of death, an assassin, and Hammershield had met his price. Mister Clay Brentwood, Texas Ranger would be dead long before he reached Dallas.

CHAPTER TWO

-

A few minutes before six pm, Clay Brentwood was sitting on a bench outside the train station. The wind had died down and shop owners were trying to clear up the debris blocking the street and their doorways.

Clay was smoking a cigarillo and trying to relax, which wasn't working very well. He was wondering how he would go about tracking down and capturing Aaron Hammershield. The man would not be easy. Hammershield liked playing the cat and mouse game and he was usually two or three steps ahead of the law, which is why he'd never served any prison time.

"Mind if I share your bench?" a drummer in a derby hat asked.

Clay looked up at him and said, "It's ah public bench," gesturing toward the empty space.

The man sat down and stuck out his hand. "Looks like we'll be traveling together. My name is Tyrone Brewster. I sell women's under garments. Are you married?"

"No. I'm a widower. My wife died a few years back," Clay said with sadness in his voice.

Brewster lifted his hat and said, "My condolences, sir."

Clay nodded.

The man who called himself, Tyrone Brewster, stared at Clay, thinking, 'I could kill him right here and be done with it. It would be easy,' but decided there would be too much of a risk of being seen. He would stick with his plan, which he considered to be foolproof. Besides, he was in no hurry. He had all night and he preferred killing his victims when they least expected it and in no position to fight back.

They sat in silence for several minutes before Brewster asked, "What takes you up to Dallas, business or pleasure?"

Clay thought it strange. Out here, people didn't ask personal questions unless you were the law, or a close friend and this man was neither. Maybe it was because he was from back east somewhere. Drummers were known to be talkers and maybe that was all it was. "No business, just a pleasure trip. My sister is getting married and she asked me ta come up for the weddin'," Clay lied, looking directly at the drummer for the first time.

Suddenly, the hairs on his neck were standing on end. There was something about the look in the drummer's eyes that he just plain didn't like. The man's eyes had a vacant stare that made chills run down his spine.

After a moment, Clay admonished himself. He hadn't even been on the job a full day yet, and he was already readin' sign that probably wasn't there.

"A wedding you say. Well now, I just might have something she'd like to take on her honeymoon," Brewster said, reaching for his bag.

Clay raised his hand. "Just keep that stuff in your satchel. There's nothin' in that bag that I would be givin' to my sister, honeymoon or not."

"But sir…"

Before the drummer could raise an argument, they heard the train whistle and felt the ground tremble as it pulled to a stop in front of the station, which ended their talk about women's under garments. They waited while eleven passengers got off before boarding the train, themselves.

Clay showed his ticket to the conductor, who escorted him to his sleeping berth, which wound up being a lower one. Clay tossed his grip on the bed, thanked the conductor and gave him a tip as the man who called himself Tyrone Brewster, stepped past them and went on down the passageway, taking note of the number on the berth.

The dining car was crowded by the time Clay got there and he was asked to share a table with two other men, ranchers from down around San Antonio, who were on their way up to Kansas City for a cattle convention. The conversation was light and Clay enjoyed talking about ranching, horses, and cattle, which was what he was doing before Curly Beeler and his gang of cutthroats raided his place and changed his life.

After supper, they went to the bar. Both ranchers planned to play cards and do some drinking long into the night, but one drink was enough for Clay. He wanted to be alert when he got to Dallas. He might get only one shot at capturing Aaron Hammershield, and he wanted ta be bright eyed and bushy tailed when he did it.

Clay was about to head for his sleeping berth when a man wearing a bandana over his face entered the car, holding a pistol in his hand. His jeans and shirt were worn and dirty and his hair hung loosely down around his shoulders. He had on a black hat that had seen better days. The man's boots were run down – and the cold look in his eyes told him this was a man who was desperate, a man who had lived on the wrong side of the law far too long.

"Put your hands in the air where I can see 'em!" the man yelled.

As the people began to raise their hands, Clay noticed the gun hand nervously moving from side to side, ready to shoot the first person that threatened him. He would have to be careful of this one; the man was scared and could explode at any moment.

Clay stood up and walked toward the man, his gun hand hanging loosely just above his own gun.

"Hold it right there, mister. If you don't want ta be shot, just raise your hands up where I can see 'em," the outlaw said, pointing his pistol in Clay's direction. "You can be the first one to donate to our cause. Now put all your money here on the bar," he said, indicating a spot near him.

Instead of reaching for his money, Clay stopped and just stood there, staring at the young man. The outlaw swung his pistol and pointed it directly at Clay's stomach.

Clay looked at him and said, "Don't do anything stupid, son, "I'm a Texas Ranger and I'd be obliged if you'd lay that hog-leg on the bar and raise your hands. I don't want to kill you."

The outlaw stared at Clay with fear in his eyes, then fired at Clay with a quick shot that seared a ridge along the left side of Clay's stomach.

With lightning speed that people in the car would talk about for years to come, Clay drew and fired.

The force of Clay's forty-four slug slammed the outlaw back against the door he'd come through. Then without ceremony, the young outlaw slid to the floor, a small trickle of blood running down his forehead, dripping from his nose - a blank, empty look in his dead eyes.

Just as Clay dropped his pistol back into his holster, someone yelled, "Look out behind you!"

Clay moved to his right and spun around, grabbing for his gun, which probably saved his life. Even so, he felt pain as a bullet ripped a hole in his left shoulder. The roar of the second outlaw's big pistol filled the inside of the train car with the smell of gunpowder.

As he was falling, Clay saw the second outlaw. The man was pointing a gun at him, ready to take a second shot. Clay fired from mid-air and saw the man's eyes go wide as the bullet tore into his stomach.

Clay landed hard but rolled over and came to his feet. The man had an angry look on his face and raised his pistol, trying for another shot, but before he could squeeze the trigger, a second bullet from Clay's pistol slammed him in the chest, knocking him backward. The outlaw's grip on his pistol loosened and the gun fell to the floor of the train car, followed shortly by the dead outlaw.

Alert for the possibility of more outlaws, Clay glanced out of the window and saw a rider leading two horses at breakneck speed, trying to keep up with the train.

Clay walked to the door, stepped over the dead outlaw and went out onto the small landing. He took aim and fired his big forty-four pistol, and watched as the rider's hat flew off into the air.

The man leading the horses yelped and immediately turned off to the side and without letting up his pace, raced away from the railroad tracks.

Upon returning to the inside, a portly gentleman dressed in a dark suit approached him and said, "I'm a doctor. John Clemmons out of Dallas. Come over to the bar and have a seat. Let me see what I can do about your wounds, it's the least I can do for what you did for us.

When Clay was seated at the bar, men came over and patted him on the back, offering to buy him drinks, but he accepted only one, a double. The raw whiskey helped dull the pain in his shoulder and side.

By the time the doctor finished bandaging his wounds, the conductors or someone had carried the dead bodies away.

The doctor offered Clay a small bottle of laudanum to help with the pain, but Clay had heard stories about how the stuff was addicting and politely said, "No thanks."

The conductor saw him to his berth and repeatedly told Clay if there was anything he needed, just ask. The railroad was indebted to him.

Clay thanked him, assuring him he was fine and was relieved when he finally left.

After half an hour of tossing and turning, his mind a turmoil of thoughts, wondering if this part of the country would ever become civilized, he got up and walked down to the end of the car and opened the door. A cool draft of air met him as he stepped out onto the landing and lit a cigarillo. The sky was cloudless and full of bright, twinkling stars. Clay never seemed to get tired of looking at a sky filled with its millions of lights. It made him feel small and vulnerable, yet curious about the wonders of it all. The rocking back and forth along with the steady clickity clack of the wheels against the rails, had a soothing effect on him.

Clay finished his cigarillo and figured maybe he could go to sleep now. His nerves had settled down some and the pain in his side and shoulder was tolerable. Besides, his eyelids were getting heavy.

He turned and started to open the door when the sound of three rapid gunshots rang out. Looking through the window of the door, he saw a man standing next to his berth with a pistol in his hand, and the hand was pointed toward the inside of his sleeping area.

He couldn't see the man clear enough to identify him, but whoever it was, was dressed in the uniform of a conductor. "Now why would one of the conductors be tryin' to kill me?" Clay asked himself out loud.

Ignoring the pain in his side and left shoulder, his adrenaline kicked in and he was about to draw his gun and go see who this would-be killer might be, when the man turned and started walking rapidly in his direction, shoving the pistol under his coat.

Clay stepped to the side and waited.

When the man came through the door and was about to step across to the next car, Clay grabbed him by the shoulder with his good arm and spun him around. "You lookin' for me?"

For a moment, Clay couldn't believe his eyes. It was the women's undergarment drummer, but he was dressed like a conductor!

The man's eyes grew wide when he saw Clay standing there, alive! He reached inside his coat to get his pistol, but before he could get it out of the holster, Clay smashed him in the jaw with his fist. The man's head went back, pain racing through his brain and his knees began to buckle. He struggled to maintain his upright position by grabbing Clay's injured arm.

Clay tried to ignore the pain in his shoulder, but the truth was he almost fainted from the severity of pain that raced to his brain. Jerking back to free himself, he unintentionally gave the man who called himself Brewster, the opening he needed.

Brewster slammed his knee into Clay's groin and heard him expel an oath as he was doubled over by more pain.

Satisfied he was in control, again, Brewster drew his pistol and turned it in Clay's direction.

Bent over like he was, Clay did the only thing he could do. He drove his head into the man's midsection like a battering ram, knocking him backward.

In the small space between the cars, there wasn't much room to maneuver, so when Brewster was driven backward, he lost his grip on Clay's arm, and found nothing to grab hold of or stand on, but air.

The would-be assassin, felt himself moving backward, but could do nothing to stop it. Dropping his pistol, he reached for the ranger, missing him by inches, and the next thing he knew, he felt the edge of the speeding train car slam against his shoulder, knocking him away from the train.

He flew through the air a good distance before hitting the ground with a jolt; rolling over several times, then finally landing face down on the ground not far beyond the railroad tracks.

Barely able to breathe and cursing his bad luck, he lay there trying to get his wind back, watching as the train disappeared into the night.

By the time Clay was able to stand up straight, the man was somewhere back along the tracks, probably dead from the fall. He lit a cigarillo and inhaled deeply; letting the pain in his groin, shoulder and side, subside. The fight had been short and without answers as to why the man who sold women's undergarments wanted to kill him.

Suddenly, the door opened and the real conductor came rushing out onto the platform, his eyes wild with excitement. Clay looked at him and grinned.

The conductor gulped and asked, "Are you alright, sir?"

"Sure, why wouldn't I be?" Clay said as though nothing had happened.

The conductor seemed confused. "The passenger across from you said a man dressed as a conductor, fired a gun three times into your berth. Did you see or hear anything?"

"Really?" Clay said with a shocked reaction. "I've been out here havin' ah smoke. With the noise I didn't hear ah thing, and no one has come through here. Was anybody hurt?"

"Apparently not," the conductor said, scratching his neck. "After what happened in the bar, I thought, maybe…" Confused and not knowing what else to do, he said, "If you're alright, I guess I should check the other passengers in case yours wasn't actually the berth this mysterious conductor shot into." Turning, he hurried back inside the car, mumbling to himself.

Clay chuckled as he finished his cigarillo, waiting for the conductor to do his checking. Ranching had its ups and downs, but nothing like this, he thought to himself. Of course, a gnarly old steer might try ta stomp ya, but they didn't carry guns and you always knew what to expect of 'em, unlike men who tried ta kill ya when you weren't lookin'.

When he finally went back inside, everything was quiet. Without getting undressed, he went back to bed and pulled the curtain closed. Tomorrow they would find three pieces of lead in his bedding. It would be a mystery that would be discussed for some time to come. He'd like ta be a fly on the wall, so to speak, when they tried ta make sense of it all.

In a few minutes, he was dreaming of riding his black stallion and chasing wild horses across the vast plains of Texas.

While Clay Brentwood dreamed the dreams of cowboys, Aaron Hammershield was enjoying a glass of rye and a hand rolled cigar at the home of Hank Banner, a man he did business with from time to time.

Hammershield's men rustled unbranded cattle, mainly yearlings, from surrounding ranches and drove them to the Banner ranch where they would be branded, then sold under the Circle A/B brand. It was an arrangement that, so far, had worked well for both of them. The ranchers could complain all they wanted, but unless they had proof, there was nothing the law could do. And anyone who might have seen something was planted somewhere out on the prairie, the grave trampled by a herd of cattle walking over it… No witness, no evidence.

Hank Banner had a concerned look on his face. "I received a telegram from a friend of mine down in Austin. The telegram said a Texas Ranger by the name of Brentwood is headed this way, looking for you? Is he going to be a problem?" Banner asked, refilling their glasses with rye.

"No," Hammershield said, nonchalantly.

"What does that mean?" Banner asked as he took a sip of his rye.

Hammershield blew out a smoke ring and said, "You aren't the only one with friends in Austin. An associate of mine sent me a telegram that said Brentwood would be coming by train, but not to worry, he wouldn't make it."

"How can this person be sure?"

Aaron Hammershield grinned and took a sip of his rye. "First, I trust the man who sent the telegram, and secondly, the man has never failed at an assignment."

"An assignment?" Banner's eyebrows were raised.

"Yes, I hired the man a week ago to take care of Brentwood. He's been a thorn in my side far too long, and there's none better at eliminating thorns than the man I hired."

"He's really that good?" Banner asked, skeptical of the man's supposed reputation.

"You ever need somebody taken care of, let me know. I'll introduce him to you," Hammershield said with a smile. "Like I said, he's never missed an assignment."

Hank Banner raised his glass in a toast as he eyed Aaron Hammershield. This was a man he could make money with, but not trust. He just may need the services of this man Hammershield was so fond of if things didn't pan out.

Hammershield returned the jester, thinking it wouldn't be long before he wouldn't need Banner's services anymore, and he knew just the man to take care of it for him.

Far in the distance, a coyote sang his mournful song to the moon, then sat back and waited for a response that never came.

CHAPTER THREE

-

Clay was up at five. The dining car was still setting up when he entered. He'd no more than sat down and pulled off his hat when a cup of coffee was placed in front of him.

"Your breakfast will be here shortly, Mister Ranger Man," the porter said, showing a mouthful of white teeth. "On the house, sir, because of what y'all did yesterday. Ain't nobody gonna ferget that, no sir, not ever. Whoee, you sure is fast."

Embarrassed, Clay nodded and accepted the meal, which was more than he would have ordered. There were three fried eggs, fried potatoes, biscuits and gravy, a large slice of ham and a cup of coffee that he could not seem to empty.

Being polite, he cleaned his plate and left a large tip before leaving the dining car feeling like a hog ready for slaughter. He knew he couldn't eat like this all the time and expect to ride a horse any distance, let alone capture outlaws.

At seven-thirty, he stepped off the train in Dallas. The air was still cool and fresh as he walked out in front of the train station where several men with horse drawn buggies were waiting to take folks wherever they wanted to go.

A skinny little man wearing loose baggy pants, a loose-fitting shirt, and no hat to cover his balding head, stepped up to Clay and asked, "Need ah ride, mister?"

"Marshal's office," Clay answered.

"Yes sir. That'll be two bits, sir."

Clay tossed his saddlebag onto the passenger seat and stepped up and sat down next to the driver.

The driver was about to protest when he saw the ranger's badge pinned on Clay's shirt. "You after somebody, Ranger?" he asked conversationally, his blue eyes twinkling with curiosity.

"You could say I have business here in Dallas, or you might say I'm here on a pleasure trip. On the other hand, I might just be passin' through," Clay said with a wide grin. "You pick the one you like best."

The driver nodded his head. He didn't know why the ranger felt he had to be secretive about his business, but he wasn't about to ask any more questions.

Dallas was a bustling community – people coming and going. Everywhere he looked, a new building was going up. This was going to be a big city, someday, Clay thought to himself as the buggy rolled down the dusty street. A nice place to visit, but he wouldn't want to live here, too many people, and all crowded on top of one another.

Ten minutes later, they pulled up in front of a two-story building that looked fairly new. There was a sign posted on the outside wall that read, from top to bottom, City Jail, Marshal's Office, and County Clerk. An arrow indicated the marshal's office was just inside the front door and to the right. Clay handed the man four bits, twice what he'd asked for. "You've never seen or heard of me," Clay said with a serious tone and stern look in his eyes.

"Never seen or heard of you," the driver said as Clay grabbed his bag and headed for the marshal's office.

Clay chuckled to himself as the man drove away. He would be conjuring up all sorts of things to tell his comrades about having a mysterious Texas Ranger in his cab.

-

The room was not large, but large enough for a desk, three chairs, a potbellied stove, a coat rack and a chest of drawers that Clay assumed held the marshal's paperwork. On the wall behind the desk was a large board that held at least ten wanted posters – but none with Hammershield's name on them. The wall facing the street had a large window that overlooked the outside.

The marshal was of medium height, maybe five foot nine, but slightly on the heavy side. Too much deskwork, Clay decided as the man stood up and approached him.

"Marshal Billy Bob Hamson," the marshal said, sticking out his hand. "What can the city of Dallas do for the Texas Rangers?"

Clay shook hands with the man and was impressed at the strength of the handshake. "I was sent here by my boss, Bill McDaniel – the man you sent a telegram to, sayin' Aaron Hammershield is, or was here in Dallas. I got paper on him and was sent to take him back to Austin. Would you happen ta know if he's still around?" Clay said, getting right to the point.

"Coffee?" the marshal asked as he headed for a large coffee pot sitting on a stove at the far side of his office. 'No lollygagging with this ranger, he comes right to the point, the marshal thought to himself. He liked that in a man. But why was his arm in a sling that looked like it was fairly new?

"If you've got some ta spare," Clay said. "Never turn down ah cup of coffee."

The marshal poured two cups and they sat down in chairs in front of the marshal's desk.

After the marshal blew on the steaming coffee and took a sip, he looked directly at Clay and said, "Can't say I know the man, but I know who he is, or says he is, and as far as I know, he's still in the area. If he's not here in town, I can tell you where you might find him."

Clay sat up a little straighter in his chair. This just might be easier than he thought. "I'm all ears," he said, taking a sip of his own coffee.

"You the only one McDaniel sent to arrest him?" the marshal asked.

"That would be correct. Why do you ask?"

The marshal set his cup on his desk and turned back toward Clay. "Well, number one you seem to have only one usable arm, and the other is because the man is slicker than grease. I've been trying to get something on him ever since he came into town several weeks back. A man with only one arm is at a huge disadvantage any way you slice it."

Clay sat still, sipping his coffee, watching the veins on the marshal's forehead stand out, then nodding toward his injured arm, he said, "Minor skirmish on the train ride up here. Nuthin' ta be worried about."

The marshal shook his head. He'd heard these rangers were tough men, but trying to arrest a man like Aaron Hammershield all by himself and with only one good arm? He hoped McDaniel knew what he was doing. "The bank was robbed a few days ago and they got away with fifteen thousand dollars, and not a trace of evidence to follow up on."

"And nobody saw a thing." Clay said.

"Now that's the thing," the marshal said. "It took place on a Sunday mornin' while most folks was in church. While they were engrossed in what the preacher had ta say, a loud explosion just about knocked the church off its foundation, and when they ran out into the street, they saw the new mercantile store was on fire!"

He took another sip of his coffee, then continued. "While they were busy puttin' out the fire, and without then knowin' it, the bank was robbed. Probably set the explosions to go off at the same time, and while folks was concentratin' on the fire, they robbed the bank and then disappeared like a whiff of smoke.

"Although I can't prove it, I have reason to believe the men who robbed the bank work for Hammershield. Also, there have been three men killed in the alleys up in Frog Town after winning big at the poker tables. Everthing I know tells me Hammershield had his hand in that, too, but I haven't been able to come up with even one ounce of evidence against him. He always seems to have several of his, so-called business associates hangin' around him; bad men with reputations as gun totters, but no paper on them in Texas, who swear to his whereabouts at the time of the crime."

"Never at the scene of the crime and always has an alibi," Clay said with a grin. "Sounds like Hammershield alright."

"That describes him to a tee," the marshal answered.

"Don't reckon I need any more evidence. I've got enough paper on him ta see him hung several times," Clay said, patting his shirt pocket.

"During the day, if he ain't asleep in one of the whore's rooms in Frog Town, he's out at the Banner place. Hank Banner is another one

I'd like to see behind bars. He claims to be a cattle rancher, but never has any cows grazin' his range, exceptin' when our local ranchers come up missin' their unbranded yearlings. Of course, all the cattle he sells, has the Circle A/B brand on them and they're not worked over brands either. Nobody has yet ta come forth sayin' they seen anything, but we've had several cowboys come up missing. Some say they drifted, but I don't buy that. I think they saw something and was killed, then buried somewhere out there on the prairie, but I ain't found no graves, at least not yet."

The marshal took another sip of coffee, cleared his throat, then said, "At night you can usually find Hammershield at one of the gambling places in Frog Town, playing poker. Says that's how he makes his money. But the word is, he ain't that good ah player."

"Is this Frog Town someplace near here?" Clay asked, having never heard of it.

"Red light district, in the north part of town, along the river. Can't miss it," the marshal said, gesturing with his hand.

Clay nodded his head. "And this Banner fella and Hammershield are thicker than flies on ah watermelon?" Clay asked.

"Right, again," the marshal said with a grin.

"And where might this Banner ranch be located?" Clay asked, making mental notes of everything the marshal said.

"East of here about five miles. Take the road east out of town and you'll top over a hill that overlooks a wide valley. Ranch house, barn, corrals and such will be off to your left, less than a mile from the road. Banner owns about three thousand acres over that way."

Clay drank the last of the coffee and stood up. "When I catch up to Hammershield, can I depend on you for accommodations in your jail until I can book tickets back to Austin?"

"It will be my pleasure. But watch yourself. He has a lot of associates who might not like him being arrested," the marshal said, shaking his head.

Clay was not surprised and would keep a wary eye out for the trouble he was sure he would find. Sticking his hand out, Clay said, "Thanks, I'll keep that in mind. Since it's still mornin' and I have some time ta kill, I plan ta ride over and check out this, Banner ranch. Like ta go along?" Clay asked to see how much sand this marshal had.

"Wouldn't want it any other way," the marshal said. "Truth be told, I've got a couple of horses down at the livery stable that could use some exercise."

Clay had the feeling he and the marshal were gonna get along just fine. Besides, it would be easier havin' somebody along who knew the lay of the land, and an extra gun hand could mean the difference between livin' or diein'.

Thirty minutes later they were headed east, riding two sorrels that acted like they were happy about getting out in the open. Clay's mare kept pulling at the bit, wantin' to run, and he was tempted to let her. It felt good to be riding again. All this train travelin' and fancy vittles lately was beginin' ta make him feel a mite soft around the girth.

During the ride, the marshal couldn't hold back any longer and asked Clay about his injury, and Clay filled the marshal in on what had happened to him.

When Clay finished, the marshal shook his head, and said, "In case you need to spend a few days here in town, you know, to rest up some, I'd recommend you try ah room at Ethel Perkin's place. She runs a boarding house here in Austin, mainly for long-term boarders. The lady spreads a good table and the place is clean. The price is a little high, but worth it. I know this for a fact cause that's where I live."

"Widow lady?" Clay asked.

"Ahhh, not exactly." the marshal said, scratching his ear. Grinning, he said, "The place used to be ah house of ill repute. Ethel was the madam. Seems she let herself fall in love with this drummer fella who ran off with one of her girls. She took it right hard and shut the place down, then left town. She was gone for a few months; nobody seemed to know where, but when she came back, she was a changed woman. She turned the place into a sixteen-room boarding house and changed her profession from madam to that of a respectful woman who takes in boarders. It was tough at first, but she was well liked and after awhile folks sorta forgot about her past. That was over ten years ago. She don't talk about it, but I heard someone say that during the time she was gone, they saw an article in a newspaper down in New Orleans about a drummer and a pretty young gal bein' shot in their bed on one of them big paddle wheel boats."

"Well, I'm not one ta judge folks," Clay said with a grin. "If you recommend the place, then I reckon if I need ah place ta hole up for ah day or two that is clean and serves good vittles, that's where I'll go."

As was his custom, Clay kept a constant vigil on the land around him, even while he was talkin'. A man couldn't be too careful. Even a tiny slip-up could mean the difference between seein' another sunrise or never seein' another sunset.

They came to the top of a rise and hauled up, allowing their horses to blow. The sun was shining brightly with a few stray white puffers floating slowly across the sky. Clay took the time to look the land over and what he saw was cattle country. It reminded him of his own ranch. The knee-high bluestem and prairie grass waved back and forth in the wind like waves on the ocean. There were clumps of elm and Texas ash, with some stands of pecan trees scattered about.

It made him wonder why this Banner fella wouldn't rather be a legitimate rancher instead of runnin' with the likes of Aaron Hammershield and his bunch. Sometimes, folks were just plumb hard ta figure out. The one thing he did know about outlaws, they was always lookin' for fast, easy money without workin' none too hard for it.

Off to the left, less than a mile, Clay could see the ranch house, corrals and barn.

"That's Banner's place, down there," the marshal said. "What's the plan?"

Clay thought for a minute, watching a cloud formation that reminded him of a big ole bull buffalo. Finally, he looked at the marshal and said, "I reckon we'll just ride down to the house and knock on the door, and if he's there, I'll arrest him."

The marshal looked at Clay and said, "I surely do hope you know what you're doin'."

"So do I, Marshal, so do I," Clay replied as he touched the horse in the sides with the heels of his boots, not wantin' the marshal to see his nervousness.

As they rode toward the Banner place, Clay felt the tension begin to build inside him. Hammershield was not a man to be underestimated and the man had reason to hate him. Hammershield had gone to great measures to extract money from Clay, only to have the tables turned on him, costing him thousands of dollars. And that wasn't a thing that sat well with him. At least that's the way he would see it, Clay guessed.

As they rode along, the marshal studied Clay. The man had sand, he had to give him that. He just hoped the ranger wasn't being stupid, riding in bold as brass like he owned the place, especially with only one good hand. On the other hand, surprise might be the best approach. Maybe he could get the drop on Hammershield and there would be no bloodshed. Not being a man who trusted to luck, he lifted the thong off the hammer of his pistol. He wanted to be ready in case things didn't go exactly as planned.

CHAPTER FOUR

-

The man who called himself Tyrone Brewster, and other names as the situation called for was by birth, John Redmond of Virginia.

John's father had been a gambler and a drunk. He was also a tyrant and his mother was anything but strong and died from too much abuse when John was eleven. For the next three years, without a wife to beat on, John suffered at the hands of his drunken father. Then one night, after one of his father's drunken tirades, John decided he had taken all the beatings he was going to take, and when his father passed out, John got his father's pistol out of the drawer where he kept it, and with trembling hands, shot him in the forehead while he slept.

He rummaged through his father's pockets and found ninety-six dollars. After saddling his father's horse, he poured kerosene over his dead father and the interior of the house and set the place on fire. At the ripe old age of fourteen, John Redmond stepped into the saddle and rode away without a backward glance. Because of his weak mother and domineering father, John held no love for his fellow man. To him, the only life that meant anything was his own.

During the next few years, he tried his hand at several things, but none of them seemed to pan out. He even worked for a while as a touring actor with a road show, which is where he learned about becoming people other than himself. But acting didn't pay much and one day a man he'd met said he would pay good money to have his rich wife killed. John saw this as a way to use his acting skills, and at the same time make some easy money. Since it wouldn't be his first time to kill, he took the job.

Dressed as a minister, John talked his way into the lady's living room, where he stabbed her repeatedly, then lit a stick of dynamite that had a long fuse and laid it next to her. He walked out of the house, got on his horse and rode away. When he finally heard the explosion, he was more than half a mile away and nobody the wiser.

That was also the day his reputation as a killer for hire began.

On his second assignment, dressed like a duke with a mustache and short beard, John knocked on the victim's front door around ten in the evening and when the man, still half asleep, answered, John shot him through the heart and walked away.

In a secluded stand of trees, on the outskirts of town, John removed his phony beard and clothes, then buried them in a hole he'd previously dug for this very purpose. Dressed as himself, he sauntered back into town and was walking down the sidewalk when the sheriff hurried past him without a second glance, running in the direction of the murdered man's house.

The murder was never solved and John Redmond's future was set. In all the years since, he had never been accused of any crime, nor had he ever been arrested – and he had never failed an assignment until he met Clay Brentwood.

Several years back, he'd met Aaron Hammershield in Little Rock, Arkansas, and was introduced by one of his other clients. Aaron had a man he wanted taken care of and John was hired to do the job, which went off smooth as clockwork. Since then, he had done two other jobs for Hammershield, which had gone off without a hitch, and now, John Redmond, alias Tyrone Brewster and other names as the situation fit, was the only one Hammershield hired to do his dirty work for him.

When things had gone sour in his attempt to kill Clay Brentwood and he'd been thrown from the train, he thought he was going to die without completing his mission; but as luck would have it, he wound up only bruised and mad as ah bull bein' castrated.

Limping and furious, he made his way to the road running parallel to the railroad tracks and hadn't gone more than half a mile when a man on horseback came riding up behind him.

Seeing a man limping down the road this far from town, made the rider curious. The man's clothes were torn and he seemed to be in bad shape. Being a compassionate man, he stopped, which as it turned out, was not the best decision he could have made.

John lured the man into stepping down from the horse by faking more pain than he really had, and while the man was still halfway out of the saddle, John stuck a knife between his ribs.

He went through the man's pockets and found twelve dollars in cash, a timepiece and papers that identified him as Randal Hoffsteder, a circuit preacher. He put the money in his pocket, rolled the man into the ditch and threw the identification papers in after him.

"Being a man of the cloth didn't do you much good, did it, preacher man?" he said as he mounted Hoffsteder's horse and rode away to the north. Dallas couldn't be more than a day's ride.

Dallas being a growing town, he figured he could hide out somewhere for a few days until he felt better, and then hunt down Brentwood and kill him. He had never failed a kill and he wasn't about to start now. John Redmond wanted no flaws on his resume.

The following morning, John stopped in a stand of pecan trees to let his horse rest a moment while he stepped down to relieve himself. He'd just climbed back onto the saddle and was about to ride on when two men topped over a hill not far away.

John couldn't believe his luck; there he was; not more than a few hundred yards away, and ripe for the killing. But having no rifle, only a knife and derringer, all he could do was watch as Brentwood and another man rode off to the north. "I wonder where they could be going?" John said to himself.

John waited a few minutes, then rode over to the spot where the two men had stopped. He could see Brentwood and the other man heading toward a ranch house in the far distance. Stepping down from the saddle, John Redmond picketed his horse where it couldn't be seen, then removed his hat and lay down on the side of the hill where he could keep watch and at the same time, get some rest.

-

Clay and the marshal rode into the yard of the Banner ranch, easy and peaceful like. Clay looked around, taking in the scope of things. There were no ranch hands or other signs of much use. In his way of thinking, even a small rancher should have a hand or two about the place. He could see only two horses in the corral, and no sign of a buggy, which is what the marshal said Hammershield used.

They rode slowly up to the front of the house and was about to step down, when a man of around forty stepped out of the door with a double-barreled shotgun pointed in their direction.

Dressed in a white shirt, dress pants and store-bought shoes; the man looked more like a shopkeeper than he did a rancher, especially a small rancher who had to do his own work. The man was clean shaven and building a paunch around the middle. In Clay's opinion, the man looked far too soft to be a rancher; plus, he had shifty eyes and a hard mouth.

When the man noticed the marshal, he lowered the scattergun. "Didn't know it was you, Marshal. What are you doing out this far from town?"

The marshal looked over at Clay and nodded his head.

Clay nodded back and turned to the man on the porch. "Name's Clay Brentwood and I'd be much obliged if you'd send Aaron Hammershield out. I'd like ta talk to him."

"Bout what?" Banner asked.

"I reckon that would be between him and me," Clay said, nonchalantly.

"And just what makes you think he's here?" Banner shot back.

The marshal spoke up. "I know he spends a lot of time here, Hank. So, if he's here, just send him out."

"I'd do that, Marshal, I surely would, ceptin' he ain't here. Haven't seen him in a couple of days."

"Mind if we see for ourselves?" the marshal asked.

Hank Banner stepped aside and swept his hand toward the house. "Be my guest, Marshal, but only one of you."

After searching the house, barn and out buildings, Clay was satisfied Hammershield wasn't on the property.

"If he's still around, he'll for sure be in one of the gambling houses tonight," the marshal said as they topped over the hill and onto the road that led back to town.

Once again, Clay's eyes were searching the landscape, looking for anything that was not as it should be; a glint of metal, a footprint, a movement. What saved his life wasn't a glint of metal, but a slight movement and the sound of a bridle rattling.

Out of the corner of his eye, Clay detected the slight movement off to his left, just inside the stand of pecan trees and then, ever so slightly, his ears picked up the sound of a horse shaking his head and biting down on his bit. Automatically, Clay ducked forward, and at the same time, kicked his horse in the sides, causing it to lunge forward.

Jerking his pistol from its holster, he fired two shots in the direction of the sound as he raced toward the stand of trees. Someone was there, of that he was sure; possibly Hammershield. If it was him, he wasn't going to let him get away. From the far side of the stand of trees, he heard the pounding of hooves as whoever it was, rode off in a big hurry.

The marshal rode up next to him, his own pistol in his hand.

Without asking, Clay grabbed the rifle from the marshal's saddle scabbard and raced his horse toward the far side of the trees.

Coming out of the stand of pecan trees, Clay could see for several miles, but he needn't look that far. The rider was no more than a hundred yards in front of him. The horse the man was riding, was limping bad on his left foreleg. He still didn't know who it was or why the man was watching them from hiding, but the fact was, he didn't like folks spyin' on him, and he wanted to know the who and the why.

John Redmond looked over his shoulder and saw Clay Brentwood coming toward him and cursed. The man had more luck than any man should have, John thought, as he kicked the horse in the ribs, but the horse refused to be bullied and almost came to a complete stop.

John Redmond knew, limping like he was, the horse would never out run Brentwood's horse. He wasn't sure why the horse was limping; but decided one of the shots could have hit him in the leg, but stopping to investigate was not an option right now.

The only thing he could do was to do the unexpected and at the same time, satisfy his contract with Aaron Hammershield.

At that moment, the horse staggered and almost fell. Cursing, John pulled the horse to a halt and stepped down. Reaching into his pocket, he pulled out the only weapon he had besides his knife, a two-shot derringer that was only good for close work, and even then, the bullet needed to strike a vital spot. He was glad he hadn't wasted what little ammunition he had on the preacher man. Using the horse as a shield, he waited for Clay to get close enough to use the derringer.

As Clay got closer, his eyes widened in amazement; it was the drummer from the train! Clay could see no weapon, but that didn't mean there wasn't one. The man's arms and hands were hidden behind the horse.

As he got closer, he made a decision and brought the rifle to his shoulder. Taking aim, he put a bullet close to the horse's hind leg.

Already wounded, the horse shied and leapt forward, leaving John Redmond with nothing to hide behind.

The man stood there, exposed. He had no weapon showing that Clay could see, but that didn't mean he didn't have a hideout gun. Most killers did. Even though this man had tried to kill him, and would try again, Clay couldn't shoot the man down in cold blood. All he could do is arrest him for attempted murder.

John Redmond stood very still, his hands to his sides, the derringer slightly behind his right leg, hidden from sight.

Clay stopped his horse ten feet away and started to step down, keeping his eyes on the man who called himself, Tyrone Brewster.

Keeping his head, Redmond just stood there. He wanted to kill Clay Brentwood so bad he could almost taste it, but he had to wait until he was certain of a kill.

Before Clay's foot touched the ground, and he was still slightly off balance, Redmond lifted the derringer and fired it at Clay.

Again, it was Clay's quick reaction that saved his life. Seeing the man's arm come up, Clay pushed away from the horse and fired the rifle from the hip, like a handgun. The rifle bucked in his hand and the roar echoed off across the wide valley.

A small piece of lead from Redmond's derringer whizzed past Clay's head so close he felt the wind from it, followed an instant later by a sting as a second bullet dug a small furrow in the fleshy part of his right leg, just above the knee.

John Redmond had gotten off two quick shots with his twenty-five-caliber derringer; one miss, and one connecting with his enemy's leg, neither bullet doing much damage.

The bullet from Clay's rifle lifted Redmond off his feet and knocked him backward. He landed flat on his back with blind eyes staring at the sky. Clay's bullet had ruptured the heart of the assassin with many names and he was dead before he hit the ground.

Cautiously, Clay walked over and looked down at the man and saw a red spot on his chest that was oozing blood. He would like to have talked to the man to find out why he'd tried to kill him, but it was too late for that, now. Clay was searching the man's pockets when the marshal rode up.

"You sure make life interesting," the marshal said, stepping down from his horse. "Are you hurt?"

"Couple of scratches, nuthin' ta worry about," Clay said, grinning.

"Anybody you know?" the marshal asked, indicating the dead man.

"Met him on the train comin' up here from Austin. Said he sold women's undergarments. Called himself, Tyrone Brewster."

Clay touched his finger to the tender skin on his leg, and then said, "He's the one I told you about – the one who tried to shoot me while he thought I was sleepin'. Thought for sure the fall from the train would've killed him. Just goes ta show ya."

"Any idea why he might want you dead?"

"Only thing I can think of is, somebody hired him to send me to my maker, but I ain't sure who that somebody might have been."

"What about Hammershield?" the marshal asked, sliding his rifle back into the boot.

Clay studied that for a moment, then said, "I reckon it could' a been him, but how would he have known I'd be on that train?"

"Like I told ya, Hammershield has friends everywhere. If he's the one who hired him to kill you, we'll know for sure when we walk into the gambling house tonight and he sees you're still on top of the ground, instead of under it."

"You plan on goin' with me?" Clay asked as he pulled a leather billfold from the man's jacket pocket and found a letter addressed to a John Redmond, at a post office box in St. Louis, Missouri, along with a little over a thousand dollars. He opened the letter and read it, then handed it to the marshal. "If I had any wonders, I don't anymore."

The marshal read the letter and whistled. "Another nail in Hammershield's coffin," the marshal said as he handed the letter back to Clay. "As far as I'm concerned, that money was meant to see you dead, so you should be entitled to keep it."

Clay stared at the sky. This was blood money and he wanted no part of it. Besides, he didn't need it. He had enough in the bank in Wichita to last him a lifetime, even after rebuildin' his ranch. After a moment, he turned to the marshal and asked, "Are there any trustworthy charities in Dallas? You know, ones that don't outright steal the money, like that Soapy Smith and his bunch?"

Soapy Smith took being a con man to another level by hiring and teaching both, men and women, the art of slight of hand, three card Monty, and other games – even pick pocketing, along with land deals and any other schemes he could conjure up to fleece people out of their savings. Because the west was growing by leaps and bounds, there were always plenty of sheep to fleece, mainly in the bigger cities where there was less chance of getting caught.

The marshal grinned and shook his head. "We got several charitable organizations in Dallas, but like you say, most of them are crooked. The only one I would trust would be Father O'Brien. He runs a home for orphans and he's always in need of money and supplies – like books and paper and things."

Clay handed the money to the marshal and said, "See that he gets this. And no names mentioned, you hear?"

The marshal took the money and stared after this strange man who hunted outlaws with one arm in a sling. As far as he knew, rangers didn't make much money. So why would Clay give away more than a thousand dollars? There was more to this man than met the eye, the marshal thought as he put the money in his saddlebag.

Clay walked over and took the dead man's horse by the reins and led him back, noticing a slight trickle of blood on the horse's left foreleg. After checking, he realized one of his bullets must have grazed the horse's leg. The wound wasn't a serious one, but he'd have it looked at when they got back to town. In the meantime, he tied his bandana around the wound to stop the bleeding.

The marshal helped him load the body belly down across the saddle. The horse shied from the smell of blood, but since there was very little, he settled down quickly and allowed the dead man to be tied onto his back.

Because of the horse's injured leg, the trip back to town was slow.

Neither man felt like talking much; each one absorbed with his own thoughts.

Clay was wondering how much longer his luck would last. How many times could he be shot at and not killed. As far as he was concerned, he had already gone far beyond his limit, and he wasn't looking forward to what lie ahead.

The marshal was still wondering why a man would give away a thousand dollars and not want anybody to know about it? There was so much about this man that he didn't know or understand.

On one side, he was easy going, but when he needed to be, he was as deadly fast as any man he'd ever seen, and accurate. He had witnessed that this very afternoon when Brentwood shot from the hip, using a rifle, while he was off balance in the middle of getting off his horse. There was no doubt the man had sand, and he didn't get rattled easy. When it came right down to it, Clay Brentwood was as dangerous as the men he sought and a man to give a wide berth to.

The telegram from McDaniel had said he was sending his best man, and now that he'd seen him in action, he believed McDaniel to be right. Tonight should prove interesting.

CHAPTER FIVE

-

After dropping the body off to the undertaker, and giving him ten dollars for his services, Clay took the horse to the livery stable and gave the hostler money to board the horse and tend to his leg until the rightful owner could be found.

The hostler took one look at the brand and whistled. "Know this horse," he said. "It belongs to Randal Hoffsteder, circuit preacher. Sold it to him myself a few months back. He was due here yesterday morning. You don't suppose that feller you brought in killed him for his horse, do ya?"

"That would be a strong possibility," the marshal said. "I'll ride out in the morning and have a look see." He turned to Clay and said, "Hoffsteder had no relatives that I know of, and if he is dead, the horse would belong to you."

The liveryman nodded his head in agreement.

"Let's wait til after we're sure," Clay said.

As they walked away from the livery stable, Clay looked at the marshal, "Now about that boardin' house you've been braggin' about."

What neither Clay or the marshal noticed was the man leaned back in a chair, propped against the wall in front of the barbershop, who took an interest in their passing. He was of medium height and build, dressed in a dark suit, with a black, flat crowned, wide brimmed hat down over his eyes, but not so far that he couldn't see. The man wore a brace of pistols with shiny walnut handles and the guns were tied down in the gunfighter style. He watched them until they were out of sight, then got up and followed them at a safe distance.

When they got to the front of the boarding house, Clay stopped and whistled. It was not only big, but also well maintained. It had a white picket fence and roses were planted all around the yard. There was a white rock path leading up to a wide veranda type porch, where several rockers rocked back and forth in the late afternoon breeze.

"Like I said, Ethel Perkins runs a clean boarding house, and serves good meals," the marshal said, patting his growing midsection.

The marshal had told him Ethel Perkins was around sixty, but when she opened the door, he took a step back. She was still a fetchin' woman with soft brown eyes that could melt ah man's heart. Her long, auburn red hair was streaked with white here and there. Her hair was neatly combed and she had a white ribbon pinned on each side close to ear level. She reminded him of a much younger woman; one with a figure that filled out a dress in all the right places.

After introductions were made, the marshal added, "I know you don't usually take overnight guests, but I was wondering if you might make an exception this one time."

Ethel looked at Clay and liked what she saw; plus, she didn't care for the likes of Aaron Hammershield. Of the sixteen bedrooms, two of them were empty right now. "Of course. For you marshal, anything," she said, patting his cheek. "Supper in about an hour."

Clay unpacked his small bag, cleaned the wound on his leg and then dropped down on the bed and was asleep in less than a minute. Ah smart man caught a little rest when he had the opportunity.

His eyes opened with a start; his hand reaching for the pistol lying next to him when he heard footsteps approach his door.

"Shake a leg, ranger. Supper in five minutes." Ethel's voice was rich and pleasant as she tapped lightly on his door.

"Save me a seat," Clay called out as he swung his legs over the side of the bed, wincing from pain in his leg.

The dining room was possibly the largest room in the house. Three long tables, seating six people each filled the center of the room. Food was laid out on a long table against one wall. There was a large bowl of golden fried chicken, a bowl filled with mashed potatoes; and three bowls with handles on them filled with white milk gravy. Further down were bowls of green beans, beets and fresh rolls. At the end of the table sat three apple pies, with ladles of cream sitting next to the pies. On a small table next to the food table were two silver urns; one with coffee and the other iced tea. Where she got the ice, Clay didn't know and didn't ask.

Several people already had their plates in their hand and were standing in line, including the marshal. Clay picked up a plate and got in line behind a tall man in a dark suit and sober look, who turned out to be the undertaker, Zebedia Black. Zebedia nodded and said, "Nice to see you again, Mister Brentwood."

Clay nodded and asked, "You live here, too?"

"Yes," Zebedia said as he began to put food on his plate. "My room is nice, the food is the best in town, and the landlady is… well, need I say more? Where else could a man get all of this for four dollars a day?"

At first, Clay had thought it a mite expensive, but the way the undertaker said it, it didn't seem so bad.

When he'd loaded his plate, he sat down next to the marshal. Knives, forks, cups and napkins were already on the table. He was about to get up and get himself a cup of coffee when Ethel reached across and filled his cup from a smaller silver coffee pot she was carrying. "Just one of the many services provided here," she whispered as she whisked past and began filling the marshal's cup, her perfume lingering in his nostrils.

Clay smiled as he placed this information in the back of his brain. She had a way of making a man feel relaxed, which is something he had rarely done during the past three years. He leaned forward and was reaching for his coffee when the window exploded and a bullet seared the back of his neck.

Everyone left their seats and dove onto the floor. Everyone that is, except Clay and the marshal.

Clay threw himself backward and at the same time fired three quick shots at the window and heard a yelp.

Together, he and the marshal ran for the front door and raced outside just in time to see a horse and rider wasting no time hightailing' it around the corner of a building up the street, the sound of a horse running full out lingered in the air.

"Recognize him?" Clay asked.

"Sorry, I didn't get ah good look. Are you alright?"

"No, he's not!" Ethel's voice rang out. "He's been shot in the neck!"

In all the excitement, Clay had forgotten about the burning sensation in his neck.

On the way back inside, Ethel noticed Clay was limping slightly. "Did you get shot in the leg, too?"

Clay grinned. "That happened earlier today," he said, meekly.

Ethel shook her head, giving him a questioning look. "Will this country ever get civilized enough to where people won't go around shooting at each other?"

"We can only hope," Clay said as he entered the house and followed her to her living quarters in the back of the house.

The room was large and elegantly done. From where he sat on a stuffed chair, he could see a bedroom that looked to be equally large and lavishly furnished and wondered what it would be like to spend some time there?

Ethel was a good nurse. With a practiced hand, she bandaged his neck, his chest, his shoulder and his leg. She was all business and didn't respond one way or another when he had to drop his pants so she could work on his leg, although he did notice her eyes straying from time to time.

She used some kind of salve that took the sting away, and covered each one with white gauze. Clay decided he would need a tin of that to put in his saddlebag. Especially since everyone seemed hell bent on shooting him every time he turned around. When he asked about it, she handed the can of salve to him and said, "Keep it, I have more."

Afterward, he thanked her, apologized for the window, and gave her money to have it repaired, along with a few dollars for patchin' up his wounds.

At first, she declined the offer, but at his insistence, she relented and took the money.

Clay left, noting that nothing about the bedroom had even been suggested. The woman had class.

-

At nine o'clock that night, Clay met the marshal in his office and together they walked up the street to Frog Town. Clay was wearing a clean sling. His clothes covered his other wounds. Walton's Saloon and Gambling House was ablaze with lights and tinny piano music.

As they walked through the front door, a young woman of about twenty stepped up next to the piano and began to sing a slow, melancholy song. The place was crowded and noisy, but when she started to sing, all talking stopped. Every man in the place turned and stared at the young woman. Women were scarce in the west and were treated with respect, especially the young, pretty ones, and this one was all of that.

Clay had to admit, she was very pretty with her raven black hair, large dark eyes, white teeth, and rosy red lips that looked like they yearned to be kissed. She was about five feet two and had a petite figure, and the icing on the cake was, she had a better than average voice. She was the center of attention and she knew it.

When she glanced his way, she smiled, and winked. Clay put two fingers to the brim of his hat and nodded. She would definitely be a temptation, but he wasn't interested in the female gender right now, he was here on business.

Clay's eyes automatically began to scan the room for Aaron Hammershield, and when they found him, the man was sitting at a poker table toward the back of the room.

He was dealing cards and had his back to Clay. Clay touched his elbow to the marshal's arm and nodded in Hammershield's direction.

Everyone's attention was on the young lady singing and paid scant attention as the marshal and ranger made their way toward the poker table at the back of the room. This is too easy, Clay thought to himself. The hair on the back of his neck was standing on end, which told Clay to stay alert, things might not be as easy as they seemed.

Aaron Hammershield felt a presence and looked over his shoulder. Surprise filled his eyes and he sighed. "You must have the luck of the Irish, Mister Brentwood. I would have bet money that you would be dead by now."

"And you'd know all about that, wouldn't you?" Clay said, tossing the letter on the table.

Aaron Hammershield glanced at it and smiled. "You do get around, don't you? You've come a long way from a man found guilty of murder and sentenced to hang to becoming a Texas Ranger. I guess it does pay to have money."

The marshal got a quizzical look on his face. Had he heard right? Brentwood had been sentenced to be hung for murder, but instead, he became a Texas Ranger? That had to be a humdinger of a story. One he was sure he would like to hear.

Ignoring the remark and the look on the sheriff's face, Clay decided to get right to the reason he was here.

"Aaron Hammershield, I have a warrant for your arrest. I'm taking you back to Austin to stand trial for the murder of Jake Comers and Julio Flores, and for breakin' outta jail to evade justice," Clay said as he'd been taught when making a formal arrest. "And, just so you know, I'll be filin' charges against you for attempted murder for hirin' ah man ta kill me. Now, are you comin' peaceful like, or do I get the pleasure of messin' you up a bit before I take you in?"

The piano player stopped playing and the room became graveyard quiet. He and the young lady were both staring in the direction of the poker table, ready to dive to the floor should lead begin to fly. Everyone knew of Hammershield's reputation but knew nothing of this upstart of a Texas Ranger who might be facing his last day on this earth.

Hammershield laid his cards on the table, then picked up the glass of whiskey sitting near the cards. He took a sip, and then said, "At the moment, you have the upper hand, but know this, Mister Texas Ranger, arresting me is one thing, but getting me back to Austin is a whole different matter."

Clay stared at Aaron Hammershield and knew the man spoke the truth. The room was full of men ready and able to assist him with no more than a word. He would not only need to be cautious, but maybe hire a couple of deputies. He wondered if the state of Texas could afford it or would he have to pay for them out of his own pocket?

Hammershield scooted his chair back and was about to stand up when the man in the dark suit stepped forward. "You want I should do away with this tinhorn ranger, Mister Hammershield?"

Clay had noticed the man standing nearby, but hadn't taken a hard look at him, he had been too absorbed with Hammershield; a mistake he wouldn't make again.

The man was of average height, with ice-cold eyes and a square jaw. He wore a black hat with a silver hatband. He was well dressed and the walnut handled pistols looked to be oiled and ready for use. The holster rig, tied down in the gunfighter style, looked to be handmade and well exercised.

The gunfighter stood ramrod straight, glaring at Clay. Everything Clay knew about his type was personified in this man. He would be fast and deadly, of that there would be no doubt. All Hammershield had to do was nod and the ball would be opened. He didn't want a shootout here in the saloon, but he may not have a choice.

Clay glanced around and saw a wide berth had been given behind him and the young gunfighter. The other walls were crowded with at least twenty men and a few women of the night, all watching and waiting.

Clay pulled off his sling and tossed it to the sheriff, then faced the young gunslinger and said, "You got a name young fella? I hate killin' a man whose name I don't know."

The young man got a surprised look on his face. He wasn't expecting Clay to stand up to him. The ranger looked like he might be an interesting challenge, but he wasn't worried. He knew there was nobody faster than him and killing this ranger would just enhance his reputation; plus, Mister Hammershield would pay him handsomely.

"Since you're going to be the one who dies, my name won't matter much; but if you want to go to wherever it is you go when you die with my name on your lips, so be it.

The name's Bennett, Lance Bennett and I'm going to kill you. Draw!"

The young man was fast, very fast, but his gun was only half way out of the holster when Clay drove his fist into the young man's wind. Air rushed out of his mouth and he doubled over in a surprised meeting with Clay's other fist as he swung a hard uppercut to the man's jaw. The blow straightened him up in time to see a third blow coming toward his face. His eyes went blank and in slow motion he sagged to the floor.

Clay had just reached down and pulled the twin pistols from the gunfighter's holsters, when the young singer screamed, "Look out!"

Clay reacted by turning to his left and at the same time, bringing both pistols to bear on a man with a bandage on his leg, who was pointing a scatter gun in his direction.

Flame shot from both pistols at the same time, both making small holes in the man's chest area near his heart.

The shotgun slipped from the man's hands and for a long moment, he stood there, his dead eyes staring at nothing. Then, like a tree, he fell over backward.

Along with everyone in the saloon, the marshal was astonished at the speed and accuracy of Clay's two shots.

Clay looked at the marshal and said, "I'm real sorry about that, but he didn't give me any choice."

The marshal just nodded his head, still in awe of what he'd witnessed.

Clay looked at Hammershield, "If you don't have any other folks objectin' to my arrestin' you, we'll be goin' to the jailhouse now."

Hammershield gave a slight nod of his head and walked out of the saloon in front of Clay as Clay put his sling back on.

The marshal threw beer in the face of the young gunslinger and hauled him to his feet, giving him a shove in the direction of the door.

As they left, the marshal called over his shoulder. "Somebody take that dead man out of here and down to the mortician and tell him Mister Hammershield will pay the bill."

After locking Hammershield in the jail and collecting money for the mortician, he then locked the young man who called himself Lance Bennett in a separate cell and hung the key ring on a peg on the wall of the office, near the door to the cells.

"I don't know about you, Mister Ranger man, but I could use a shot and a beer," the marshal said, slapping Clay on the back.

Clay looked at the marshal and nodded. He had earned a drink. There had been some tense moments that could have gone either way. Once again, he had been lucky, but what about next time, or the next time after that?

As they left the jail and walked across the street, Clay said, "That was too easy."

"Easy?" the marshal said. "There were several of his men in the saloon, just standing there, waiting for a signal. We could have been in a small war that we might not have won. You whipped a gunslinger with your fists, and then had a shootout with a man pointing a shotgun at you. That's what you call, easy?"

"You know what I mean. I saw 'em too, and figured several of them might be ready ta open the ball and earn a little extra money for killin' me, but like many would be gun totters, they're all mouth. The two that tried thought they had the advantage against a man with only one arm."

The marshal nodded his head. "Speakin' of that, how is your arm?"

"I'm hopin' that drink we're gonna have will help take away the pain, I think I opened it up again," Clay said with a grimace.

As they stepped up to the bar, the marshal ordered two shots and two beers, and then asked, "What about now? Will they back off or come up with some plan to rescue him?"

"Based on past experience, I'm thinkin' they'll come, and I think I'd best stay the night over at the jailhouse, just in case," Clay said, downing his shot, then draining his glass of beer.

The marshal downed his drinks and ordered a second round, then turned to Clay and said, "Yeah, I think you're right, it will be good to have someone inside the jail. And based on what you told me about him breaking out of jail down in Austin, I posted two men outside with rifles in places where they can keep watch just in case they try to pull that same stunt, again."

"That's good," Clay said. "If we can make it 'til mornin', I think I can get him on the train. It's the trip between here and Austin that I'm worried about. I'm thinkin' maybe I should hire a couple of deputies to help me get him back. Know of any good men who might fit the bill?"

"Possibly the two men who are standing watch, both good men and both needing some work," the marshal said, finishing off his second drink.

Clay had not yet touched the second drink but was reaching for it when all hell broke loose. The sound of gunfire burst through the open doorway of the saloon; followed by the sound of dynamite exploding and the sound of bricks landing in the street like giant hail balls.

"Not again," Clay yelled as he dashed through the open doors, gun in hand, just in time to see a cloud of dust and speeding horses heading north toward the city limit and the open country beyond.

The marshal called out, "Andrew, Tim!"

For a long moment there was silence, then a strained voice from across the street, in between two of the buildings, called out, "Over here, I need help. I've been shot!"

They found Tim Matthews on his back, blood running from his nose and mouth. His eyes glazed over.

"Sorry, marshal, they sneaked up behind..."

Clay squatted next to Tim and checked him, then looked up at the marshal. "He's dead; shot three times in the back."

By then, several men from the saloon and other townspeople had come out to see what had happened.

The marshal appointed two of the men to take Tim Matthews to the undertaker. "Tell him the city will pay him. He'll understand."

The marshal stepped into the street and called out, "Andrew! Andrew Prine, where are you?"

A groan came from across the street and they saw a tall, skinny man in overalls come staggering from the alleyway. He was holding his head and having a hard time keeping his balance. Blood was running down from the top of his head and covering his face with streaks of red.

By the time the marshal and Clay got there, two men from the saloon were holding him upright.

"I… I saw some men ride up to the back of the jailhouse and when I stood up, I felt ah sharp pain on top of my head and that's all I remember. Did he get away?"

"Fraid so," The marshal said.

"I'm sorry, Marshal. Thought I was hid good. Where's Tim? Is he all right? I heard gunshots."

"Tim didn't make it," Clay said.

Andrew just stood there with a blank stare, like he didn't understand.

The marshal turned to the two men holding Andrew's arms. "Take him over to the doc's. Tell him I said for him to take care of Andrew. I'll settle with him later."

When everyone was gone, they looked at the damage to the jail, which was extensive. The dynamite had done a lot more damage than just blowing a hole in the wall. The building was beginning to tilt to one side and by morning it would more than likely be nothing more than a big pile of bricks and wood.

"I'm real sorry about those men, Marshal," Clay said. "Since he was my prisoner, I'll pay the doctor and undertaker, and there will be no argument."

"That's mighty nice of you, Clay. Are you rich, or something? You toss money around like you got a pocketful. I thought rangers were broke most of the time," the marshal said with a half curious smile.

"Let's just say the state of Texas can afford it," Clay said, avoiding the actual question. Now, about your jail..." he said, lifting his hand to scratch the back of his neck.

"Don't worry about it, I've been hammering the city council for a new jail for some time now. Come mornin', it'll be nothin' more than a pile of rubbish. Some of 'em will grumble but I think they'll get the message," the marshal said with a twinkle in his eyes.

As they walked toward the boarding house, the marshal asked. "What will you do now, go after them, or go back down to Austin?"

"Reckon I'll be headin' north. My boss told me not ta come back without him. Any idea where they might have gone?" Clay asked.

"If it was me, I'd want to get out of the state of Texas, and Oklahoma isn't that far away," the marshal said, matter of factly. "Ardmore is only about ninety miles north of here, and the railroad runs through there. He could catch a train from there and go north, east, or west. He could even head back down south, if he was so a mind to."

Clay stared out toward the north, digesting the information. The sheriff might be right, but on the other hand... Hammershield might have other ideas.

"You might be right," Clay said. "Then again, that might be what he wants me ta think. There are a lot of places he can hide in the Oklahoma badlands. I heard tell about the Dalton's and some others hidin' there. Hammershield's not one to leave the hen house when there are more chickens to be plucked. No. My gut tells me he won't go far."

The marshal thought for a moment, then said, "I don't envy you, you got your work cut out for you. And I think you just might be right. Hammershield will probably do just the opposite of what a man thinks he will do."

The next morning Clay and the marshal rode east, out of town, leading another horse just in case it was needed. It was pleasant, the sky was clear, and they could see for miles. A little before noon, both were riding easy in the saddle, the steady rocking motion was about to put both men to sleep, when Clay pointed to several buzzards circling overhead approximately half a mile in front of them. The marshal and Clay both kicked their horses into a run and when they got closer; they saw what looked like a pack of coyotes feeding on something. The marshal fired a round in their direction.

The coyotes ran away a short distance and milled around, yipping and nipping at each other. One, big male, raised his head and howled.

What remained of Randal Hoffsteder was not a pretty sight.

After wrapping the remains in a piece of canvas and tying it on the back of the extra horse, they headed back toward Dallas.

That night, Ethel Perkins not only redressed Clay's wounds, but spent most of the night getting better acquainted and the next morning, over breakfast, she made it plain that he would be welcome anytime he was in town.

CHAPTER SIX

-

Clay traded the horse with the bruised leg for one that had four good ones, a feisty appaloosa mare who looked like she had plenty of bottom, which he would need where he was goin'. She stood fifteen hands had good markings, but it was the look in her eyes that settled it for him. Those eyes told him she would do to ride the river with.

A few minutes after he'd loaded his saddlebags, he said his goodbyes to the marshal and hostler, and headed north in the direction of Ardmore, Oklahoma. The brilliance of the mornin' sun promised to be a scorcher. He touched his heels to the ap's side and felt her immediate response as she stretched her legs into an easy lope.

The marshal and the hostler stood in the middle of the street, watching until the ranger was out of sight.

"He made a good choice with the ap. She was one of my best," the hostler said, then spit a stream of brown liquid into the street.

"My gut tells me there's a lot to learn about that man," the marshal said, still wondering how a convicted killer wound up to be a Texas Ranger?

"That may be," the hostler said, "but he's not here ta tell us and my belly's ah growlin', letting' me know I ain't et breakfast yet. You want ta come along?"

"Had breakfast already, but a cup of coffee sounds good," the marshal said as he turned and followed the holster in the direction of the café.

-

Clay's gut told him he wouldn't be so lucky catchin' Hammershield with his guard down this time. The man would know he would be comin' after him and he would be ready.

A few miles north of Dallas, Clay decided he would let Hammershield worry a bit about where he was and what he was up to. He turned the appaloosa to the northwest in the direction of his ranch and his neighbors, the Sooners. It had been awhile since he'd seen them and he reckoned they would be happy to know he was still up and walkin' around, plus, he could tell them of this new twist fate had thrown at him. Marion would get a kick outta hearing he was now a Texas Ranger.

Deep down he knew the real reason for goin' over that way wasn't about seein' the Sooners, which would be real nice, especially since they were such good friends and all, but the truth was if huntin' down Aaron Hammershield was gonna be a long ordeal, he wanted the black stallion between his legs. The big horse was like havin' a second pair of eyes and ears. Over the years they had grown to depend on one another. Besides, he just plumb missed his horse.

The air was humid and the temperature was climbin' toward the mid-eighties and was accompanied by a hot wind that did nothing to cool things off. Every couple of hours he stopped and allowed the appaloosa to take a breather. He would pour a little water from the canvas bag he carried on the pack and let the horse drink. It wouldn't do to let his horse die out here in the middle of nowhere. Texas was miles and miles of nuthin' but miles and miles. A man afoot out here was hard pressed to survive if he didn't know how to live off of the land like the Indians did. Fortunately for him, he figured he would survive but truth be told, he didn't hanker on the long walk, especially with several tribes of hostile Indians between him and where he was headed.

While his horse was catchin' its wind, he rolled a smoke and took a minute or so to reflect on his situation. He was still a young man in his mid-thirties with enough time left to rebuild his ranch and maybe find another woman to care for; and if he was real lucky, have a son or daughter.

But first, he had to track down and arrest a man who killed without compassion; a man who was as cunning as he was mean - and not get hisself killed.

Riding directly into the setting sun, it was hard to spot a place to camp for the night, so it musta been fate that allowed him ta see the trickle of smoke just above the tops of a small stand of elm trees, off to his right.

Whoever made that fire knew somethin' about fire buildin'. To the normal person's eyes, it would probably never have been noticed, since there was little of it and it disappeared into the sky almost as soon as it cleared the tops of the trees.

Now a man out on the trail doesn't often run into many folks in this part of Texas, maybe a herd of buffalo or some antelope, or even cattle, but other than Indians, its mighty lonely country.

Still some fifty feet from the stand of trees, Clay called out, "Hello the camp. Just ridin' west when I saw your smoke. I got coffee, bacon and beans that I can share if you're ah mind to."

When there came no reply, Clay eased the appaloosa a little closer and saw a small camp fire circled by rocks and a coffee pot hangin' from a metal rod arched out over the fire, but no one in sight, which he took as a sign ta keep movin'. Whoever was camped here wasn't lookin' for company, and out here most folks respected each other's wants.

As he turned the ap's head to leave, he heard the hammer on a rifle click, loud and clear.

"Hold it right there, mister," a woman's voice called out.

'Now what would a woman be doin' out here all alone, Clay wondered? Or was she alone? Could be she was with somebody – maybe somebody who was hurt. He hadn't seen any horses so he had no idea how many people were in the camp. One thing he did know, you didn't argue when a woman pointed a gun at you, especially one with the hammer thumbed back.

"Easy now," Clay said, raising his hands. "I mean no harm. If you ain't wantin' company, I'll just keep on ridin'."

"Didn't say I didn't want company – just choosy, that's all. Now, step down and turn around so's I can get ah better look," the woman's voice said.

Clay grinned as he stepped down from the appaloosa and turned around. "From your accent, I figure you must be from Tennessee, or near there," Clay said. "Met a couple of fellas some time back from Tennessee by the name of Hacker – Ezra and Shiloh. Ever hear of 'em?"

"Can't say I know 'um personal like, but I've heard of 'um. Lots of Hackers back there. Me, I'm from Cinch Mountain. Got some Hackers there too. Fightin', drinkin' and runnin' shine is mostly what they do," the woman said as she stepped from behind a large elm tree and lowered her rifle. "You can water your horse in the pond yonder, then come on back. I was about ta fix supper."

For just a minute, Clay just stood there starin'. She was tall, almost as tall as him and filled out her jeans and shirt as well as any woman he'd ever seen. She had sky blue eyes and a spite of freckles on her nose and cheeks, which gave her a girlish look, even though the rest of her said different. She was between twenty-five and thirty, he would guess. She had on a wide brimmed hat that had seen better days and hangin' from it was the reddest hair he'd ever seen. She was carrying a Winchester rifle and had a thirty-two-caliber pistol hanging on her hip in a worn leather holster.

"Well, don't jest stand there ah gawkin'. Go water yer horse and picket her over close ta mine," she said as she sashayed toward the campfire. The swaying of her hips made it hard for Clay to concentrate.

Finally, Clay nodded and took the appaloosa's reins and led her toward the pond, and as he walked away he heard her say, "Land ah Goshen, you'd think ah man had never seen ah woman walk, afore."

It was a clear water pond, not muddy like most, about twelve feet across. He figured it must be underground fed to be so clear.

Clay went up a little ways above the mare and got down on his knees and took a sip. It was cold and sweet. When he'd had his fill, he took off his hat and washed his face and hands, and ran his fingers through his hair. After picketing his horse next to hers, he stood back and admired her choice of rides. It looked to be a Morgan of good blood, ah roan with four white sock feet and a blaze on his nose - a stallion that stood a good sixteen hands.

"He's as good as they come," her voice said from behind him. "Pa won him in ah poker game when he was down in Memphis. And when ma and pa died, he became mine."

Over a supper of antelope stew, which was delicious, Clay made his condolences about her folks.

"Thank ya," she said. "Indians," she said with a bit of contempt in her voice. "At least that's what I was tole. But between you and me, I think it was the Mullins. I was away at the time and had Noble with me. That's what I named papa's horse, cause that' how he acts – ya know, like one of them uppity folks ya read about in books. Anyway, when I got back I found ma and pa layin' in the yard. They had arrows stickin' outta their backs and they'd been scalped, so's everbody thought it was Indians."

"Sounds like a reasonable assumption," Clay said, staring at her across the fire.

"Yeah, I reckon it would, but the thing that got me ta wonderin' was the fact that both the cattle and the horses were gone, and even the pigs. Now, Indians might take the horses, but not the rest. And y'all can bet they would'a burned the place ta the ground, but it was left standin'."

Clay stared at this mountain girl and was impressed by her. She was a person who did her own thinkin', and he liked that.

"And if that wasn't enough evidence ta prove it weren't Indians, two days after the funeral, who do y'all think come ah ridin' up ta the front door, hat in hand, tryin' ta buy the place off me at half the price it's worth?"

"The Mullins?" Clay asked.

"Sure as the sun comes up ever mornin', it was them, alright. Well, it didn't take me all day ta add two and two tagether. No sir! I grabbed my rifle and pointed it directly at ole man Mullins and said, "You take you and yourn and get off my land and if I ever see y'all on it again, I'll consider y'all ta be trespassers up ta no good, and I'll start ta loadin' ya down with lead. Now git! And thet's jest what they did."

Clay refilled their coffee cups and squatted back on his heels. "If I may be so bold to ask, what brought you out here in the middle of Texas? Did somethin' happen?"

The woman stared at him across her cup and after a moment, she said, "Us Bensons ain't never had much but the land. That's my name, Benson. Loralie Benson. Anyway, all we had was the land, three thousand acres of the best timberland on the mountain, and that's why the Mullins wanted it. They figured ta cut it down and get rich.

"But pa, he didn't think that way. He liked the mountain jest like it is. We raised horses, and cattle that grazed the mountainside, kinda wild like. Pa would break a few horses ta sell down at the bottom, along with some of the cows, as money was needed."

"Do you still own the land, or did somethin' happen to it?" Clay asked.

"I still own the land and will till my diein' day. But I need money ta restock the place and I ain't about ta cut down no trees and sell 'em ta do it."

"Then how do you plan on doin' it?" Clay asked, still trying to figure out what she was doin' out here, all alone.

"Gold," she said matter of factly. "I heard there was gold in the mountains of Colorado. Heard folks was ah pickin' up nuggets big as yer fist by jest wadin' out in the river and stoopin' over."

Clay chuckled, then turned serious. "Yes, there is gold in Colorado, but more go bust lookin' for it than those who find it."

"You tellin' me it ain't true thet I can jest walk out inta ah river and pick up enough ta rebuild my place?"

"No, I'm not sayin' that at all. You might be one of the lucky ones. I only know that when I went up there ah few years back, after almost a year, and after payin' for grub and tools, I came back with eighteen dollars. And durin' that whole time I only heard of one man who struck it rich. That's all I'm sayin."

They talked long into the night about life and the struggles man goes through. Clay told her about his wife and unborn child and all that had happened since.

"So, you don't really want ta be ah ranger?" she asked.

"No ma'am, I'm just a rancher at heart. And when my time is up, I've got the prettiest piece of land a man could ever want to go back to. And like you, I'll have to rebuild it, but that won't be a problem. I've got a little put away."

The following morning, they said their goodbyes; she was headed northwest and he was headed west.

After giving her directions to his ranch, he said, "Whatever happens, I'd like to hear about it. And if you're ahmind, and have the time, it would be my pleasure if you'd drop by for a visit."

Before she rode off, she smiled and said, "I jest might do that, Mister Clay Brentwood, Texas Ranger, I jest might do that."

He watched her go until she was silhouetted against the horizon, and for some odd reason, he felt like he was losing something special.

Shaking it off, he rode west, suddenly in a hurry to get to the Sooner ranch.

He hadn't gone yet a mile when he heard gunshots coming from the direction Loralie Benson had ridden. Whirling the ap, he put his heels to her sides and raced off in the direction of the gunfire, which by now, sounded like a war goin' on.

In the distance, Clay could see the telltale smoke of gunfire rising into the air and urged the appaloosa to run a mite faster. He just hoped he wasn't too late. A woman was at a disadvantage out here alone. He knew he should have ridden a ways with her, at least as far as where she could meet up with other people.

Topping over the ridge, Clay saw three Kiowa Indians on horseback, circling a ditch. Two Indian ponies had trotted away from the fracas and were feeding on the long grass. Two dead Kiowa Indians lay sprawled on the ground.

Getting closer, he raised his Winchester and fired from the back of his horse and saw a brave knocked from his horse. And as he was swinging for a shot at another one, he heard her rifle sound off and watched as another brave was knocked from his pony.

The last brave yelled something at her and turned his horse and fled toward the nearby hills and safety.

Clay rode up to a small ditch and stepped down. Loralie's big Morgan was lying on his side at the bottom and Clay thought he might be dead, until she said something over her shoulder and the horse rolled over and stood up, shaking hisself.

Loralie looked over at Clay and said, "Thank ya kindly fer comin' on the run like ya did, but ya didn't have ta, there was only five of 'em."

"To most people, five would have been five too many, especially Kiowa, they're known to be fierce fighters," Clay said, marveling at the strength of this woman from Cinch Mountain. She had stood against five Kiowa braves and had downed three with the expertise of a seasoned Indian fighter.

He wondered what they were doing so far south, but reasoned they were known to ride a far piece to raid the white man.

Leading her horse, together they climbed out of the ditch and walked up to Clay. She dropped the reins and stepped closer to Clay, then reached up and kissed him on the mouth.

Clay's heart began to pound and he felt the blood rushing to his brain. The kiss tasted like fresh honey and lasted not near long enough.

Loralie stepped back and smiled. "That was jest my way of sayin' thank-ye," she said. After shoving her rifle into its boot, she swung onto the saddle without using the stirrup, then looked at Clay and said, "Your ah good kisser, Mister Ranger man. You keep ah lookout, ya hear, cause one of these days I jest may be callin' on yer place fer that visit you offered."

And before he could say anything, she rode away, waving.

In the distance, Clay saw the lone Kiowa brave sitting on his horse waiting for Clay to leave the battleground. When it was clear, he would return and collect his brother warriors and take them home for a proper burial.

His head was still spinning when he mounted his horse and turned her nose toward the west, having feelings he hadn't felt in a long, long time.

Clay shook off the feeling. They had nothin' in common. She was a mountain woman who only came west to find gold so she could go home and rebuild what someone had taken from her. With a chuckle he realized they did have somethin' in common. Both of them wantin' ta rebuild somethin' that was taken from them. The kiss had only been her way of sayin' thank you for helpin' her out of a tight situation.

"Besides, what would she want with a flatlander," he said to the appaloosa. "She likes the mountains and I like the wide-open plains of Texas."

That night, he dreamed of them riding together. One minute they were racing across Texas like they were runnin' from a tornado, her long red hair streaming behind her; then suddenly, the dream changed to them standin' on ah mountain top, holdin' hands and lookin' down at ah lush green, tree filled valley.

The appaloosa snorted and stamped her hoof, bringing Clay out of his dream. His hand closed onto the forty-four at his side and he looked around without sitting up. From over near where the appaloosa was picketed, he heard the growl and rolled over, coming to his feet in one smooth motion.

Dropping the pistol on his bedroll, Clay grabbed the Winchester and raised it to his shoulder, just as the cougar leapt toward his horse, his front claws extended.

The shot from Clay's rifle caught the big cat in midair and drove it sideways. Clay could tell the cougar was dead by the way it landed and stayed still. The bullet had entered right behind the left front leg and punctured the heart.

The appaloosa was still nervous and skittish when Clay dragged the cougar away a good distance. With some gentle talk and a handful of dried apples, the horse settled down and Clay was able to fix some breakfast.

After a pan of fatback and beans, downed with black coffee, Clay headed west and felt the morning sun, warm against his back as it climbed over the horizon.

Alone, out in the middle of nowhere, riding across the vast prairie, a man could feel at peace with the world. There were no outlaws ta chase, no young hotheads bracin' you for ah shootout. It was just you and your horse, and the wide-open spaces.

CHAPTER SEVEN

-

"You really are a Texas Ranger?" Rebecca Sooner asked as she refilled Clay's coffee cup.

Clay swallowed his mouthful of steak and beans. "Yes ma'am, I really am ah Texas Ranger, at least for now. The judge said it was that or get my neck stretched."

"I've just never thought of you as a Texas Ranger before," she said with a giggle. "You're much too nice."

Seeing Clay's face turn red, Marion interrupted. "So, if you bring Hammershield in, then McDaniel will talk to the judge about reducing your sentence?"

"That's what he told me," Clay said; taking a sip of coffee, glad Marion had changed the subject.

"And how long do you suppose that will take?" Marion asked.

Clay studied on the question for a bit, then said, "Don't know; maybe a week, maybe six months, maybe never. Why do you ask?"

Marion grinned. "It's comin' up on time to take some beeves up to Wichita. Heard the market is strong now and since it was your bull that helped build the herd, I figure half of them are yours."

"You do, huh? When do you plan to make the drive?" Clay asked.

"Not for a few weeks yet. Several of the other ranchers plan on makin' the drive, too, thought we might bunch them together for safety. I was kinda hopin' you might want ta go along."

"That's mighty generous of you my friend," Clay said, "and I would like to help if I can. As far as those cattle go, they're all yours. I was lucky the bull was here when Curly and his bunch raided my place. He can help me get ah new start when this is all over. As to helpin' with the drive, Hammershield has to be my number one priority. Keep your fingers crossed that I catch him soon and can get back here in time ta tag along."

"You got an idea where he might be?" Marion Sooner asked.

Clay laid his knife and fork down on the table, wiped his mouth on the cloth napkin Rebecca had given him, and took a sip of coffee before he answered. "My gut tells me he's holed up somewhere in the badlands of Oklahoma, which means he could still sneak out and do his business in both, Oklahoma and Texas, or maybe even go over to Arkansas or up to Missouri, and then back through Kansas. He's got a lot of choices, along with at least a dozen places in the badlands where he can hole up and be hard ta find."

"So, you don't think he took the train to Denver or Kansas City?" Marion asked. "Seems odd. The man could go almost any direction from there and he'd be hard to follow."

Clay looked at Marion and said, "Oh, he could'a done that, alright, but I don't believe he did. He needs ta prove he's smarter than me. It's a game with him; and if he can keep on killin' and robbin' right under my nose... well then, he'll figure he's beat me, and that's what he wants. It's an ego thing with him."

"You really think he's that conceited?" Marion asked.

"If you knew him like I do, you'd think the same way," Clay said, standing up. "That's why I came here ta see you and Rebecca, and get Midnight. If I'm gonna go traipsin' all over the badlands, I want a horse under me I can count on."

At the door, Clay turned back toward, Rebecca. "Thank ya kindly for supper, Rebecca, the best I've had in some time."

"There's cherry pie," she said, wondering why he'd gotten up from the table before she'd served dessert.

"Maybe later," Clay said. "Right now, I need ta get reacquainted with a certain black horse you got out there in the corral."

Rebecca watched him go and turned toward her husband. She had a worried look on her face. "Hasn't he been through enough, already? Why couldn't that judge just have turned him loose? He only killed those men because they killed his wife. Wouldn't any man do the same?"

Marion pulled his wife down on his lap and hugged her. "Honey, I understand your worry and I'm in agreement with you, but there's nothing we can do, except pray he finds this Hammershield fella, and takes him back to Austin. Then maybe, he can come home."

"But if this Hammershield is as wily as he says, and if Clay isn't watchful every minute," Rebecca burst into tears.

"Hey, Clay is a mighty tough hombre, and pretty wily, himself," Marion said, as he held her close. When finally he released her, he said, "Now go wash your face. You don't want Clay seeing you with tears running down your cheeks."

Rebecca stood up and nodded her head. "I know he can take care of hisself, I just worry about him," she said, then turned and headed for the kitchen.

As Clay walked toward the corral, the sun was halfway over the horizon. Long shadows danced across the ground like will-o-the wisp ghosts. The black horse raised his head and looked toward the man walking in his direction and snorted. Then all of a sudden, he began prancing around like a young colt, bucking, throwing his head in the air and whinnying.

When Clay opened the gate and stepped inside the corral, the black stallion ran toward him at breakneck speed, sliding to a stop just in front of him.

"Hello, Midnight," Clay said, reaching up and stroking the horse's neck. "I told you I'd be back." Reaching into the pocket of his jeans, he pulled out an apple and fed it to his best friend.

After eating the apple, the big horse shook his head up and down and then laid his chin over Clay's shoulder.

Rebecca came out onto the porch where her husband stood watching the reunion.

"Maybe that horse will settle down now that Clay is back," Marion said.

Rebecca smiled and shook her head from side to side. "I never knew how close a man and a horse could be until I saw these two together."

-

The following morning, using the Appaloosa as a packhorse and possible second horse to ride, if needed, he thanked the Sooners for their hospitality and headed northeast for Ardmore, Oklahoma, the black stallion glad to be out of the confines of the corral.

After a few miles, he turned off to his left and crossed the invisible border between his ranch and the Sooners. It had been several years and he needed to see it – to see Martha's grave and make sure it had been taken care of.

As he rode across the rolling plains of his land, Clay marveled at the tall grass, waving in the breeze, and the size of the herd of cattle grazing off to his right. Marion Sooner was indeed doing well. This was land where they could raise some mighty fine beef, along with quality horses.

An hour later, Clay rode into the yard where his house used to be before Curly Beeler and his gang burned it to the ground.

Grass had grown tall during his absence and any evidence of a house or barn was gone. He ground hitched the horses so they could graze while he looked the place over.

The water from the well was cold and sweet. He filled two buckets that were sitting nearby and carried them over to the horses. After satisfying his own thirst, he did what he really came back here to do, visit his dead wife's grave.

Unlike the yard, the gravesite had been well cared for. It was picked clean of grass and what looked like flowers picked within the past week lay near the headstone. Rebecca would need to be thanked for that. They had been good friends. After removing the old flowers, he picked a new bunch of wild flowers and laid them close to the marker.

Standing at the end of the grave, Clay took off his hat and told her everything that had happened since he'd left, and when he finished, he said, "Not sure what the future holds so I won't be makin' promises I can't keep. But I will say, if I can get this business done with, and I'm still able ta sit ah saddle, I'll be back. This is my home and I don't want ta live anyplace else."

-

That night, just before sunset, Clay camped near a small stream and was skinning a deer he'd shot earlier when four Comanche Indians rode up and sat looking down at him. He hadn't heard them approach, and cursed himself for letting down his guard. He glanced up at them but made no move to pick up his rifle. Instead, he kept skinning his deer. From the corner of his eye he noticed they all carried carbine rifles but wore no war paint and made no move toward him. Clay made the sign for peace and invited them to step down.

Without a word, they got off their horses and led them to the stream and let them drink, then picketed them nearby.

Clay continued to work on the deer, but kept a wary eye on them. When he finished, he cut off a small chunk of meat and hung it over his campfire to cook.

The four braves were still standing at the far edge of the camp, staring at him in silence.

With hand signals, Clay indicated for them to take the rest of the meat.

Over roasted chunks of deer meat, they filled their bellies. None of the Indians spoke a word while they were eating. There would be time for talking when their bellies could hold no more. An Indian might not eat but every few days, so when food was available, he ate his fill.

Clay finished his meat and poured a cup of coffee, then sat off to the side and marveled at how much each one could eat. They didn't stop until there was nothing left but a pile of bones. When they were finished, they got up and went to the stream and drank and washed their face and hands.

When they came back, one of them picked up the deerskin and held it up. Clay grinned and motioned for him to take it. The brave nodded and took it to the stream to clean.

The tallest one, a man with a look of nobility and who looked to be the leader, pointed at the cigarillo Clay was smoking and indicated he'd like one.

During all this time, not one word had been spoken, so, when the tall Indian finished his cigarillo and spoke, Clay was surprised. Not only could the man speak English, but also knew Clay's name.

"You gone long time, Clay Brentwood."

"Yes. Yes, I have been. How do you know my name and that I've been gone?" Clay asked.

"The Comanche know many things. We watch when you come to this part of our world. We see what you did for black horse. That was good thing and I tell my brothers, this Clay Brentwood, he ah good man."

"Have we ever met?" Clay asked. "You look familiar."

"Many moons ago, during cold time, you rode into our village. You had three deer and one wild boar on your packhorse. You left all in front of my lodge. Our eyes met, but no words were spoken between us. Then you turned and left. You were very brave to come into our lodge alone. The Comanche respect bravery. From that day, my people believe you to be a man of strength and courage."

Clay stood up and stuck out his hand in friendship. "I just figured you folks could use some meat, that's all. It was a cold winter and meat was scarce, but I thank you for your friendship. I'd be honored to know your name and how you come ta speak English as good or better than me."

"I am called, Running Coyote. I am sub chief of our people, and the others are," he said pointing to each one as he spoke, "Horse Who Bites, Brave Eagle and the one cleaning the deerskin, is called He Who Sleeps A Lot."

Clay nodded as each name was spoken. "And where did you learn to speak English?"

"Many years ago, a white trapper rode into our lodge. Like you, he was not afraid to come alone. We were surprised when he spoke to us in our language and told us his God told him to come to us, find a wife and teach us the ways of the white man so we could live in peace with each other. He stayed with us seven winters before he said it was time for him to go. He got on his horse and rode away with his squaw, three sons and three daughters. We never learned his white man's name, only the name we chose for him, Man Who Sings, for he taught us many songs."

The next morning, Clay fixed enough bacon and beans for everyone, and when he'd loaded his gear and was ready to leave,

Running Coyote came up to him and said, "We will ride with you today. There are Kiowa nearby and we are at war with them. They are not real people, like the Comanche, and they do not like whites."

Clay nodded his thanks, thinking on the Kiowa braves who had attacked Loralie.

Around noon, Clay saw a small herd of buffalo and shot one, then offered it to his new friends.

After eating his fill, he left them and continued on. He had several miles to cover before nightfall.

The country he rode through was basically flat with small hills here and there that were covered with scrub trees, but not much grass. Occasionally, a ditch would loom up in front of him that would run for anywhere from a hundred feet to a quarter of a mile long and ten feet deep, like the earth had just opened itself up, yawned and gone back to sleep.

In the near distance he saw a hill rising out of the ground, maybe a hundred feet high that had a small stand of pecan trees. Thinking that might be as good a place as any to spend the night, he headed toward it.

He was no more than a hundred yards from the stand of trees when he saw the sun reflecting off metal in several places, and all close together. Without consciously thinking about it, he reined the black stallion to his left and touched his boots to the horse's sides, gripping the lead rope to the appaloosa tighter in his fist.

The black stallion responded as though he could read Clay's mind and jumped into a hard run, racing away across the barren land. Sensing the excitement, the appaloosa leaped at the opportunity to run and followed close behind the black horse.

Clay felt the sting of the bullet creasing his left shoulder before he heard the report of the rifle. Looking back over his shoulder, he saw approximately ten Kiowa braves coming out of the stand of pecans, all shouting and raising their rifles in his direction.

Looking forward, he hunted for a place to make a stand, but saw nothing but wide-open space in front of him. Alone on the big stallion, he could outrun them, of that he had no doubt, but leading a packhorse, that was another matter altogether. She was a runner, but she also carried a heavy pack. Should he let go of the lead rope and race to safety, letting them have the appaloosa, or try to find a place to make a stand, he wondered? He hated to lose the appaloosa and all the gear she was carrying.

Another bullet sped past his head and he was about to let them have the appaloosa when the black stallion made the decision of whether to run or stand and fight when he whirled and raced down into a ditch no more than forty feet in length, six feet wide and about five feet deep.

Clay let go of the lead rope and grabbed for the rifle in the scabbard tied to his saddle.

Stepping down, he leaned against the edge of the ditch and took aim.

The Indian in the lead screamed as he was knocked from the back of his horse. The others reacted by turning their horses and riding out of shooting range in two directions.

Clay looked back over his shoulder and saw both horses, drinking from a small pool of water in the bottom of the ditch.

"You have more sense than I do, big fella," Clay said before looking back to see what his enemies were doing.

They were just sitting on their horses, staring in his direction. That they would come after him, he was sure. It was the when, he wasn't' sure about. Glancing back, Clay saw water seeping from the ground, refilling the small pool. "Well, at least I have food and water," he said to himself.

When he looked again, they had gotten off their horses and were making camp. He could see the small glow of a fire they'd built. How they'd done that so quickly, he wasn't sure, but they had. Would they wait for night and try to catch him asleep? He didn't know. He'd heard Indians wouldn't attack at night because they feared if they should die, their souls would get lost and never go to the great hunting grounds. On the other hand, he'd heard it depended on the Indian and whether they believed all that nonsense. Either way, it was going to be a long night.

As the sun dipped beyond the horizon, Clay made his own fire and brewed some coffee. While chewing on a piece of jerky and sipping his coffee, he kept an eye on their camp.

They were sitting around a small fire, talking as though they hadn't a care in the world. Several times he heard laughter. Clay rested the rifle on the side of the ditch and took aim. It would have to be a very lucky shot at this distance and decided not to waste the lead. He counted nine. Not the best of odds. If they wanted to, they could come at him from four different directions and he wouldn't stand a chance.

A quarter moon and slow-moving clouds replaced the sun. He could still count nine braves sitting around the fire when the hairs on the back of his neck stood on end. He looked over and watched as both horses' heads came up, looking in the direction of the far end of the ditch. Whirling, rifle ready, he saw Running Coyote sliding over the edge of the ditch, followed closely by the other three; all carrying rifles.

"We hope you have much ammunition," Running Coyote said, as he stood up from his bent over position.

"Got enough," Clay said as he reached out and clasped Running Coyote's hand. There was no need to ask where they'd come from or how they knew he was in trouble. It was enough to know the odds had just turned in his favor.

It was close to midnight when He Who Sleeps A Lot touched Clay on the shoulder and whispered, "They come."

Clay hadn't been asleep, just resting his eyes, and was instantly alert.

"They come from all around," he whispered again. "Three from front, three from back, and one from each end of ditch. They leave one with their horses. If you take this side of ditch, I will help Running Coyote on the backside of ditch. Horse Who Bites is at that end of ditch," he said, pointing, "and Brave Eagle over there, he whispered, pointing toward the opposite end of the ditch.

Clay nodded and thanked his lucky stars he'd taken meat to them those long winters ago.

A cloud passed in front of the moon. The land in front of him became dark and eerie. Clay strained his eyes to see, and as the light of the quarter moon shone down on the land again, they raised up from the ground and charged, screaming and yelling.

Sounds of rifle fire and the smell of gunpowder filled the air. Chunks of lead hit the ground in front of him while others whistled over his head. The attacking braves didn't have time to be surprised to find out that there was more than one man in the ditch, it was over that fast. Clay had dropped two of the three charging him when He Who Sleeps A Lot stepped up next to him and shot the third brave.

Brave Eagle and Horse Who Bites went immediately and checked to make sure each brave had gone to the great beyond. The last brave, the one who had stayed with the horses was nowhere in sight and had abandoned the horses, probably figuring to come back and get them, later.

After breakfast the next morning, they dragged the carcasses of the dead braves into the ditch, took rifles, knives and whatever else they wanted, then tied lead ropes to the dead brave's horses and with nothing more than a wave, rode away.

Clay stood for a long while, watching them disappear into the western horizon, glad for their friendship.

CHAPTER EIGHT

-

A quarter moon gave scant light for Aaron Hammershield to see by as he rode into the yard of a group of three cabins located in an isolated area not far from Broken Arrow, Oklahoma. The cabins were well hidden by elm and pecan trees and known about by only a few. All was quiet – too quiet. Alert for danger, he stepped down and pretended to loosen the cinch on his saddle with one hand, while lifting the thong off his pistol with the other. Warily he looked around and saw no sign of life where life should be. There were no lights in the windows or voices coming from the cabins, which made him feel on edge.

"Glad ta see ya back, boss," a tall skinny man with a droopy moustache and cold eyes said as he stepped from the shadows. He was holding a rifle, but let the barrel drop when he recognized the man who had ridden in.

Hammershield jerked around, reaching for his pistol, then relaxed and said, "Charlie Coots, damn your hide, you almost got yourself shot, but I'm glad to see someone is on the job. Here, take my horse and put him away, then come to my cabin."

"Yes sir," Charlie said, taking the reins of Hammershield's horse and leading him away.

Inside the cabin, Hammershield lit a coal oil lamp, sat down at a scarred old table and poured whiskey into a cup. He swirled the dark brown liquid around, then took a swallow. The rotgut whiskey burned his throat, but cut the dust from his parched lips and throat. He pulled a watch from his vest pocket and was checking the time when Charlie Coots came into the small cabin.

"What'er you grinnin' bout, boss?" he asked as he dropped into the chair opposite of Hammershield and poured himself a drink. "You got somethin' up yer sleeve?"

Hammershield closed the lid of his pocket watch and said, "By now that dumb ranger, Brentwood, should be on his way to Denver, thinking that's where I went."

"Why would he think that?" Charlie asked.

"Because I sent Albert to Denver on the train, using my name, and when the ranger goes looking for me, that's what the ticket taker in Ardmore would tell him, that I went to Denver," Hammershield said with a smirk on his face.

Charlie Coots shook his head in awe. "You sure are smart, boss."

"That's why you work for me, and not the other way around," Hammershield said with a tinge of arrogance in his voice.

"Like I said, I'm sure glad you're back. The men are getting' kinda restless, sittin' round with nuthin' ta do but play cards," Charlie said as he knocked back the whiskey.

"You tell the boys not to worry. We'll have a meeting first thing in the morning and I think they'll like what I have to say," Hammershield said with confidence.

After Charlie had gone, Aaron Hammershield pulled a map from the inside of his coat pocket and spread it out on the table; taking his time to go over his plan once again, just to make sure there were no hang-ups.

The following morning, nine rugged looking men eagerly crowded into Hammershield's cabin, anticipation showing in their eyes. The boss had been gone for several weeks, looking for a new caper for them to pull, one that would put money in their pockets. And now that he was back they were anxious to hear about what he'd come up with.

A blue haze filled the inside of the cabin as Hammershield sat at the table, drinking coffee and smoking a large, foul smelling Mexican cigar. He grinned as he watched them come in. They were nine of the toughest men he could find – men who had lived outside the law so long there was no going back, and as long as he kept putting money in their pockets, they would follow him into hell and back, if that's where he chose to go.

"I understand you boys are getting tired of having nothing to do but play poker."

To the man they all nodded and grumbled something that meant they agreed. A lanky, rawboned Indian who went by Kiowa, stepped up close to the table and glared down at his boss. He was probably the only one of the group Aaron Hammershield was afraid of. The man was a killer and made his own way. Hammershield looked up and grinned, but saw no smile on the Indian's face.

"You have something for us that will put money in our pockets?" he asked

"I do, and I think you're gonna like this one; should put a couple of thousand in each of your pockets."

"How many men I have to kill for this?" the Kiowa asked.

"Hopefully, none," Hammershield said with a nod of his head.

The small cabin erupted with shouts. Some were doing a little jig, while others pulled their pistols and shot holes in the ceiling; all except the Kiowa, who stood by silently, waiting to hear what the new source of income would be without killing somebody.

Finally, Charlie Coots waved his arms to get them to quiet down, then looked at Aaron Hammershield and asked the question they all wanted to ask. "So, what's the plan, boss?"

Hammershield tossed his cigar butt on the floor and crushed it out with the toe of his boot, then reached across the table and picked up a long piece of brown paper that had been rolled into a cylinder. He unrolled it across the top of the table, putting a tin cup on each corner to hold it flat.

The men crowded around behind Hammershield as the Indian opened the door of the cabin to let out the smoke that was making him cough, then moved to a spot where he could see.

What the men were looking at was a hand drawn map of a street running down the middle of a town. Two of the buildings had x's on them.

"Gentlemen, and I use the term loosely," he said with a chuckle. "This is the main street of Fort Smith, Arkansas, two days ride from here. They have a bank loaded with money. That will be our first target."

"What'ya mean, our first target? How many we gonna hit?" Charlie asked.

"Only two," Hammershield said. "The second will be a Wells Fargo office in Fayetteville, Arkansas. They will be holding twenty-five thousand dollars, just waiting for you to drop by and pick it up."

The room was immediately filled with questions. Aaron Hammershield raised his hands and said, "Quiet down men. When you see what I have in mind, and how easy it will be, you'll be ready to go when I give the word.

After detailing his plan, which sounded just like one they'd pulled a short while back, the men shook their heads, admiring the genius of the man they followed.

"Kiowa, you and Charlie stay here while the rest of you make sure the horses are taken care of. I want them well fed and rested. And you'll need to get a good night's rest, too. We leave at daybreak."

CHAPTER NINE

-

Dirty and tired from the scorching heat and long days in the saddle, Clay arrived in Ardmore, Oklahoma hoping the information he would find would allow him time to take a long, hot bath, change into clean clothes and eat a decent meal – and maybe even have a cold beer or two. The only thing that would prevent him from doing that would be if Hammershield was still in town, which he doubted, if he even came here to begin with.

He wasn't sure yet whether the local law would be of any help to him. Hammershield may have paid him off to keep his mouth shut. It wasn't unusual to find local sheriffs under the control of some outlaw gang, especially since many of them were ex-outlaws themselves, just hiding behind a badge to keep from going to jail. A few dollars here and there, bought a man a lot of leeway.

He was surprised to see so much hustle and bustle. They were still rebuilding from the fire a few years back that nearly wiped the town out. Ardmore was still a small town that survived because the Santa Fe Railroad ran through it, allowing a person to make connections for places, like, Denver, Wichita, Kansas City and all points beyond. Ardmore was becoming a tourist attraction and people came here to gawk at the home of William M. Dalton, of the famous Dalton gang. The story was; a posse shot him down during an attempt to flee his home. If Clay could remember right, that would have been a few years back, in eighteen ninety-four.

Clay shook his head. People came from all over and would actually pay good money just to see the spot where a man was killed.

Clay rode up to the front of the train depot and stepped down, dropping the black's reins to the ground, knowing the big stallion would not wander off. The appaloosa would stay with the black stallion so there was no need to tie her to the hitch rail, either. Clay loosened the cinch and pack straps on each horse respectively, then walked them over to the nearby watering trough and let them drink.

The ticket taker was a small, rotund man of about sixty, who was mostly bald, except for the hair growing close to his ears and the back of his head. He wore a dirty white shirt, a black vest and black pants. Clay couldn't see the man's shoes, but he imagined they were black, too. On the counter was a nameplate with the name, Henry Snipes, written on it.

Henry Snipes looked up from what he was doing and saw the ranger badge. "Yes sir, ranger, what can I do for you today?"

Clay grinned. The Ranger's badge sure made folks sit up and take notice. "Just a little information, Mister Snipes, just a little information."

"Be glad to help if I can," Henry said standing up a little taller, pushing his five-foot one-inch height to its fullest.

Clay stifled a grin and asked, "Do you remember hearing the name, Hammershield mentioned around here during the past few days?"

Henry Snipes drummed his finger on the side of his face for a moment, then his eyes lit up and he said, "I did. I surely did. Just a couple of days ago two men came in, but only one of them bought a ticket. Let me see," he said as he thumbed through some papers. "Yes sir, got it right here. The man bought a ticket to Denver."

"And just how would you know the man who bought the ticket to Denver was named Hammershield?" Clay asked with a puzzled look on his face.

"Heard the other man call him by that name. I surely did... Mister Hammershield is what the second called him."

"You wouldn't happen to remember what the two men looked like, would you?"

Henry tapped two fingers of his left hand against his lips as he drummed the fingers on his right hand on the counter. Suddenly, he stopped and looked at the ranger. "By golly, I do. Mister Hammershield was taller than you, dressed in denim pants with worn looking chaps over them. He had on a red shirt that was kinda sun faded, and he was wearing a wide brimmed hat. Had a scar down across his… his, left cheek." Henry grinned at Clay and asked, "Does that help you any, Marshal?"

"And the other man?" Clay asked, laying a silver dollar on the counter.

"Oh yes, I almost forgot. He was short and kind of raggedy looking, if you know what I mean. He had the good start of a beard, and brown teeth because of the tobacco he chewed. No hand gun that I could see, but he carried a rifle of some kind. I'm not good with guns, so I don't know what kind it was. And he had mean looking eyes, I remember that."

Henry grinned at being able to remember the two men and describing them. "Hope that helps," Henry said, eyeing the silver dollar.

"More than you know, Henry, more than you know." Clay tossed a second dollar on the counter and left the depot, a slight grin growing on his face.

Outside, Clay tightened the cinch and pack straps, then mounted the black and headed for the livery stable. Tonight, both he and his horses would have a good meal and get some rest. It was just like he figured; Aaron Hammershield was still in the area.

The man at the front desk of the hotel looked up at Clay with distaste. Another cowboy who will drink too much and land in jail for fighting or some other ungodly thing and not have enough to pay his room rent. They were all the same, uncouth, barbaric creatures hardly more intelligent than the animals they rode. Well, from now on they would have to pay in advance or they wouldn't get a room. When he'd graduated from hotel school back in Chicago, he never dreamed he would wind up in this remote part of nowhere, but when he got his assignment, his instructor had said he would love the west.

"Do you have baths, and maybe a laundry? I apologize for the way I look; been on the road for some time and I'm lookin' forward ta feelin' clean, again. I'll need a room for a couple of days."

The man behind the counter almost fainted. A cowboy who wanted a bath instead of whiskey? "Yes, yes, we have both. The room is a dollar a night, the bath is fifty cents and the laundry will be a dollar."

Clay laid four dollars on the counter and as he signed the register, he told the hotel clerk he would also like a shave.

"Yes sir, coming right up," he said, ringing a bell setting on the counter, noticing for the first time, the ranger badge pinned on the man's shirt.

A Chinaman in his mid-forties appeared almost by magic, and when he was told to take good care of "Mister Brentwood," the Chinaman bowed several times, then picked up Clay's saddlebag and said, "Prease to follow me."

They went down the hallway almost to the back of the hotel before the Chinaman turned and entered a door.

Clay followed him and found himself in a large room that had several curtained off areas, another part of the room had laundry tubs where women were washing clothes, and on the other side, two older women were ironing.

Inside one of the curtained areas was a large tub filled with steaming hot water.

The little Chinaman bowed and said, "My name, Chow Ling, you need anything you call for Chow Ling. Now to remove clothes prease, and get into tub. My daughter, Mi, will be in shortly to help with bath and give nice shave. Clothes will be ready by time you finished with bath." And with that, he bowed his way backward out beyond the curtain.

Clay was soaking in the hot water that was scented with something that smelled like lavender when Mi came in. She commenced to wash his back with a soap filled sponge.

She also massaged his neck and shoulders, which almost put him to sleep.

It was when she walked around in front and began to wash his chest that he almost had a heart attack. He figured she was around twenty, dressed scantily, leaving very little to the imagination, and she was gorgeous. When she smiled, her even white teeth fairly shined.

She spoke not a word, nor did she make any suggestions that might be interpreted being provocative. She scrubbed him clean and then gave him the best shave he could ever remember having.

When he stepped out of the tub, she eyed him from head to toe with what seemed to be approval, then toweled him off. Bowing, she left the curtained area and returned within a minute with his clean and pressed clothes – even his boots had been shined.

Mi started to back away, but Clay motioned for her to wait. She stood quietly while Clay dug into his money belt and pulled out two dollars and handed it to her. She smiled and then bowed again as she left, giving him a slight swish of her hips before disappearing beyond the curtain.

Clay left his saddlebags in his room, which was on the first floor with a window facing the street. After combing his hair, he strapped on his money belt, then put on his hat and pistol. Before he left the room, he closed the curtains. Outside, he looked around, getting the lay of things in his mind before he headed for the saloon where he would indulge himself with a beer before supper.

-

At this time of day, the saloon had only a few patrons. In the far corner, four men were playing poker. Turning toward the bar, he noticed three cowboys at the far end, having a heated discussion, but thought nothing of it, drunks were always mouthy.

The bartender asked, "What'll it be, stranger?" eyeing the badge on his vest.

"You wouldn't happen ta have any cold beer, would ya?" Clay asked with a grin.

The bartender smiled and said, "I don't have any ice, but it is cool."

"Then I reckon I could use a tall glass of cool beer," Clay said, nodding his head.

When the bartender returned, he indicated the badge pinned on Clay's vest and said, "Sure glad you happened by, ranger. Those men down at the other end of the bar are drunk and on the verge of doing something crazy."

"Don't you have a sheriff, or a marshal?"

"We do, but he's out of town; trying to track down whoever it was that robbed the mercantile store. They got enough rifles, hand guns and ammunition to start a war."

Clay's mind immediately thought of Aaron Hammershield, but before he could voice his thoughts, a glass of whiskey was tossed into his face.

Clay turned and saw one of the men from the other end of the bar standing in front of him, poised to draw. The man was well over six feet in height, maybe as much as six feet four, and weighed at least two hundred and fifty pounds. His hands were big and knuckle scarred, like he'd been in a lot of fights. His nose was bent to one side, like a man whose nose has been broken more than once.

"I don't like rangers. I think rangers are the slime of the earth and ever one of 'em needs to be shot or hung," the man said, staring hard at Clay behind a face filled with brown tobacco stained teeth and several days growth of beard.

The bartender reached under the bar and came up with a double-barreled shotgun and cocked both hammers. "Back off, Clyde, there'll be no gunplay in here, today. You and your friends have had enough. Go somewhere and sleep it off."

It was a statement, not a question, but the big man was having none of it.

"You stay outta this, Bert. I'm gonna kill me a ranger."

"I'll not stay out of it, Clyde. This is my place and I say what goes on here. And I don't want it shot full of holes or torn up like you did the last time," Bert said with authority, lifting the shotgun to his shoulder and pointing it at Clyde.

Clay had heard enough to know this man was trouble just lookin' for a place ta happen. So, instead of arguing with him, he turned and headed for the door. He wasn't lookin' for trouble and maybe the best way to avoid it would be to just turn and walk away.

He'd taken no more than three steps when he was knocked forward from the blow of Clyde's fist. When he regained his balance and turned around, the man was standing there, his hands balled into fists and trouble written all over his face.

"You ain't getting off that easy, Ranger. You don't want to pull iron with me, so be it. Instead, I'll have the enjoyment of beating you to death, which will be a whole lot more fun than shooting you."

"I got no trouble with you, mister," Clay said. "Like the man said, maybe you've had a little too much to drink and not thinkin' straight. Maybe you should sleep it off. We can discuss this tomorrow when you're feelin' better."

"I feel just fine, Ranger, and I'm in the mood to fight, that is of course, unless you're too yellow to fight."

Backing out into the street, Clay figured to at least get outside where they wouldn't break up the inside of the saloon, in case he couldn't talk his way out of this.

Clyde Millsap stopped about four feet from Clay and called out to the people walking down the sidewalks, "Hold on folks. Come on over and watch…" He turned to look at the man in front of him and said, "I didn't get yer name. Hate ta beat ah man ta death thout at least knowin' his name."

"Brentwood, Clay Brentwood," Clay said, unbuckling his gun belt and letting it drop.

Clyde looked back at the people standing nearby and said, "Pay attention cause Mister Brentwood is about ta get the hell beat out of him."

The people stood where they were, watching, but saying nothing.

Clay was getting tired of all the talk and figured he might as well get it over with.

"Are you sure you want your friends to see you get a whippin'?" Clay asked in a casual tone.

Clyde grinned and spat into the street, then spit into his hands and balled them into fists that looked the size of hams. "So, you finally got some backbone, did you? Well then, come on, little man, let's see who gets a whippin'?"

In truth, Clay was not a little man, but with all due respect, he was only half the size of Clyde, so he would need two things. First, would be speed. He would need to hit and get back, quick. Second, he couldn't afford to take too many punches from Clyde. The man was a bruiser and probably hit like bein' kicked by ah mule.

"You sure do like ta talk," Clay said. "But unless you plan ta talk me ta death, there ain't been much action so far. Let me know when you're ready to open the ball," Clay said, dropping his hands to his sides.

"You want action, well get ready cause here it comes," Clyde said as he rushed forward, his right cocked for the knockout punch.

Clay watched him come and when Clyde swung a roundhouse at his head, Clay ducked under it and kicked out with his right foot. He felt his boot smash against the big man's shin and heard him scream as he pitched forward, face first, into the street.

Clay looked at the people standing on the sidewalk and shrugged his shoulders, as Clyde got back to his feet, his face red and flushed.

"That the best you got? Kickin' like a girl?" Clyde asked just before he rushed Clay again, only this time with his tree trunk arms outstretched.

Clay knew if Clyde ever got his arms around him, he would break his back and leave him in the street, so instead of meeting him head on, Clay stepped to the side and ducked under the outstretched arms, driving his right fist into Clyde's kidney area, then moved out of reach, circling around, looking where he might land his next punch.

Clyde went down on one knee and seemed to rest there for a moment before he lumbered to his feet again, a grin smeared across his face.

Clay was trying to figure his next move, when all of a sudden Clyde swung his left hand toward him and the next thing Clay knew, he was digging at his eyes, which were now filled with dirt.

Still unable to see, Clay felt the impact of the big man's fist against the side of his head.

Exploding lights flashed behind his eyes, followed by excruciating pain. His brain felt like it had been knocked loose, and was rattling around inside his head. The next thing he knew was when he landed on his back in the middle of the street. He couldn't breathe and he was still blind from the dirt in his eyes. Pain erupted in his left side and realized Clyde was stomping him with his boots.

Preservation, more than anything else, caused Clay to start rolling over and over, trying to get out of harm's way. With only one eye open enough to see through the tears, Clay saw Clyde coming toward him, and when Clyde tried to kick him, Clay grabbed the boot and twisted, sending Clyde head over heels into the air.

Clay scrambled to his feet and rushed over to the watering tank and splashed water on his face and eyes, clearing the dirt so he could see; then turned and walked back to face Clyde, who had now regained his feet and was raging mad.

Clay was mad, too, and this time he circled Clyde, biding his time.

Clyde, angry beyond comprehension, swung another right at Clay's head.

Clay slipped under the swing and drove his fist into Clyde's breadbasket, then swung upward with an uppercut that landed squarely on Clyde's chin.

Clyde was staggered and stepped back, trying to get his wind and shake off the lights exploding in his head.

Clay, not wanting to give Clyde a chance to recover, stepped in and kicked Clyde in the crotch.

The big man screamed and bent over, his face meeting another uppercut from Clay's fist that jarred him clear down to his heels.

Following the big man's backward movement, Clay slammed four more solid punches to his head, then one to the jaw that finished the fight and put Clyde flat of his back in the middle of the street.

The people were stunned. No one had ever bested Clyde Millsap before. Then, slowly, the clapping and cheering began, and by the time Clay turned and walked back up onto the sidewalk, people were talking a mile a minute and patting him on the back.

Clay raised his hands to quiet them and when they were quiet, he said, "When he wakes up, you tell Clyde he'd better think twice the next time he wants to beat up on a Texas Ranger. I reckon we have a bit more backbone than he might think."

To cheers and clapping – Clay, covered with sweat and dirt, headed back toward Chow Ling's. He was gonna need another bath and the use of Ling's laundry service for the second time today. He hoped there weren't any more bullies wantin' ta whip up on a Texas Ranger, it was gettiin' expensive.

CHAPTER TEN

-

By the time the sun came over the eastern horizon the following morning, Clay was a good ten miles north of Ardmore, heading toward Oklahoma City where he would refresh his supplies and hopefully find out a bit of information about the badlands and maybe even the whereabouts of Aaron Hammershield. If it was him, or the men who worked for him, who robbed the store in Ardmore, he must have some mighty big plans.

Within an hour, the sun was blazing hot and sweat was running down Clay's back. The air was humid and burned the inside of his nose.

Even with the heat, the black was enjoying the chance to stretch his legs. With an easy lope, he was eating up the miles, while the appaloosa followed along behind, matching him stride for stride. Clay figured he would slow the pace when the sun got a little higher and the heat became more intense. But for now, he would allow the horses a bit of freedom, but keep a close eye on them. Too many white men and most of the Indians he knew of would run a horse to death, but not him. Midnight was not only his main source of transportation, but also his friend. It was almost like they could feel each other's moods. And more than once, the big stallion had saved his bacon by alerting him to danger before it happened.

His eyes scanned the land in front of him, unconsciously searching for danger. His mind drifted off toward Hammershield and how he would be having a good laugh, believing Clay had been stupid enough to follow the false trail he'd laid down. Others might have been deceived and followed the trail to Denver, only to wind up totally confused and angry with themselves for being duped, but not Clay. He'd known the man only a short while, but in that time, he'd somewhat gotten to know the way the man's mind worked, which gave him a slight edge – at least he hoped so.

Clay could almost see the surprised look on Hammershield's face when next they would meet up. Only this time, if he got lucky enough to get him in irons, he wasn't about to lose him again; even if he had to shackle their ankles together.

Clay was still sore from the knock down drag out he'd had with Clyde, but figured he was better off than Clyde. Not only had he whipped the man soundly, but also the man's reputation as a bad man had been ruined in Ardmore. Clyde would more than likely leave town rather than face the humiliation.

Clay was happy for the people of Ardmore, not having to put up with the likes of him, but he also realized he now had a new enemy; one that would not be happy until Texas Ranger Clay Brentwood was six feet under. He just hoped it would be a long time, if ever, he would have to face him again. It was a big country and he would cross that bridge when he came to it. Right now, his mind was focused on finding Hammershield and taking him back to Austin, one way or another.

At the same time, Clyde was also thinking of his next meeting with the ranger and how different it would be. There would be no talking this time, no crowd of people watching, nor would there be a face to face fist fight or shootout; only the sound of his rifle when he shot the ranger out of his saddle from a safe distance, or possibly as the man walked down the street, it made no difference to him, as long as the ranger was dead and no one could accuse him of anything. In his mind's eye it was a perfect plan.

-

The people in the café were quiet all the while Clyde was eating his breakfast, afraid of what he might do if someone even snickered, and each one gave a sigh of relief when Clyde finished and walked out without paying his bill. They watched through the window as he headed for the livery stable, hoping he would get on his horse and ride away.

The owner of the livery stable was an elderly man who walked with a limp, and was called, Pop, and when he saw Clyde begin to saddle his horse, he approached him with a bill for three weeks of board and feed.

Already in a bad mood from being humiliated in front of the town by the ranger, Clyde pulled his pistol and beat the old man with it until Pop's face was a bloody mess and he was lying unconscious on the livery floor. Clyde picked up an almost full bottle of rye sitting on top of the old man's desk, took a long swig, then put the rest in his saddlebag.

Without a backward glance, Clyde stepped into the saddle and rode out of Ardmore and headed east, glad to be away from this no nothing hellhole of a town. If he stayed, he'd have to kill everyone in town for snickering at him or makin' comments behind his back. It was all Brentwood's fault and one day the ranger would pay.

Once they were sure Clyde was gone, each one of the restaurant patrons not only paid their bill, but also left an extra nickel to go toward Clyde's breakfast bill. They felt it was worth it to see the last of him. Plus, the owner being a widow woman who worked hard didn't need to lose money over the likes of Clyde Millsap.

A few miles east, Clyde was still fuming about the fight and the humiliation he'd suffered in front of the people back in Ardmore. Before the ranger had showed up, he'd been ah big man and folks stepped aside to let him pass. Now they would talk behind his back and snicker at him.

None of that would've happened and he'd still be ah feared man, he reflected, if he'd left a few days ago when he got the telegram from Hammershield telling him to meet him and his boys just outside of Fort Smith, Arkansas no later than this coming Saturday. Clyde wondered what Hammershield was up to now? Whatever it was, it must be big, or he wouldn't have sent the telegram. Clyde Millsap didn't come cheap.

Fate had a funny way of shaping things up – allowing two men, both looking to meet up with the same man, but for different reasons, to camp under the same stars, only miles apart.

That night, Clyde, a man known to be hell on wheels in a shootout or a knock down drag out, sat alone, staring at the small fire he'd built to stave off the cold night air. For the first time in his life, he had met his match and it rankled him. One side of him had to respect the ranger for not only standing up to him, but besting him in a fistfight. That had never happened before. He also wondered what the outcome would have been if they had had that draw and shoot inside the saloon? Well, it made little difference because the next time he wasn't going to take any chances. He wasn't about to call him out and get humiliated again. The next time, he would shoot him from a place where there would be no witnesses to put a rope around his neck.

After climbing into his bedroll, he polished off the bottle of rye, knowing it would take the edge off and allow him to sleep. He was tired of thinking.

-

Clay Brentwood was staring at the same stars, but his mind was a long way from the fight with Clyde back in Ardmore, nor was he thinking about Hammershield. Stretched out under his blanket, he stared at the sky and its billions of stars shining brightly. Somehow the clouds shifted and what he saw was Loralie's face smiling down at him. Why the Cinch Mountain, Kentucky girl filled his mind all of a sudden was beyond him.

Clay shook his head, trying to get her image out of his mind. He would more than likely never see her again, and if he did, she would be on her way back to Kentucky. What had he read somewhere, somethin' about two ships passin' in the night? Well that's what they were, two strangers that had met while goin' in different directions.

Why did she kiss me, he wondered? And why did it make me feel the way it did? After all was said and done, what did they even have in common? Not much that he could think of. He was a man and she was a woman and that was about it. That she was a woman to ride the river with was neither here nor there, or was it, he wondered?

Long into the night Clay wrestled with his feelings about a redheaded spitfire he hardly knew. They were two ships that had passed in the night and that was all there was to it. He knew he needed to concentrate on Hammershield and not be distracted by a woman he hardly knew if he wanted to stay alive.

-

Loralie Benson was also gazing at the same sky and same stars, only her mind wasn't on the gold she came west to find, it was on a handsome Texas Ranger who had ridden into her life like one of them knights in shinin' armor she'd read about in those books her papa used ta read from. Her papa had taught her to read and enjoy stories of people long past, such as, Faulkner, Mark Twain, Charles Dickens, William Shakespeare and several others. She had been particularly interested in the stories about men and women falling in love.

"Loralie Benson, you get ahold of yerself. Yere actin' like some silly schoolgirl. He's ah flatlander and your ah mountain girl, bred through and through, and y'all ain't got nuthin' in common," she told herself before she drifted off into the land of dreams where a girl sometimes goes.

In spite of what she'd told herself, the stranger who called himself Clay Brentwood, was there, and they were walking together, hand in hand.

Overhead, a shooting star raced across the sky, leaving a long trail in its wake, while the destinies of three unsuspecting lives was being planned by an unseen force.

CHAPTER ELEVEN

-

After a little over three days on the trail, Clay Brentwood rode into Oklahoma City around ten in the morning under the sound of rolling thunder and black cloudbanks looming ominously overhead. Lightning could be seen inside the clouds and the wind was beginning to pick up.

The city was divided by the North Canadian River and as he rode down along the south side of the river, he saw people hurrying to find shelter. One man yelled at him over the rising wind, "Better find shelter, mister, we got us a hail storm comin'."

Clay looked over his shoulder and, in the distance, he saw a wide swath of hail falling from the sky and it was headed straight toward him.

Touching his heels to the sides of the black stallion, it responded by racing toward the open portal of the livery barn as though it felt the impending storm and could read the sign overhead.

HORSES BOARDED BY THE DAY,

THE WEEK OR THE MONTH

HORSESHOEING AND BLACKSMITH

WORK DONE TO ORDER

The sign was beginning to swing violently back and forth in the heavy wind as he rode into the barn and stepped down. Hail began to rattle on the roof of the livery barn and he turned and looked toward the street. A wall of ice balls was pounding the street and buildings, some as big as his thumb.

"You made it just in time," a voice from near the livery stable office, said.

Clay looked over to where the voice came from and grinned. "Yeah, I reckon I did."

About that time the intensity of the storm increased dramatically, causing both men to jump.

"Known of men caught out in these storms ta wind up beaten to death," the hostler said.

The hostler was a large man with wide shoulders and arms that looked to be as big as a man's leg; his hands were as big as two ordinary man's hands. He had a full head of white hair that was put back in a ponytail. Though his eyes had a sparkle to them, the rest of his face looked tired. His bib overalls were old and worn, as was his cotton shirt.

His boots were rundown, but he was close shaved and his clothes were clean, as was the interior of the barn.

Clay unsaddled the black and took the backpack off the appaloosa while the holster stood near the entrance shaking his head as he watched the balls of ice pile up in the street.

Clay was giving the animals a rubdown with pieces of canvas hanging on a peg to use for that very purpose when the holster turned and walked over to where Clay was tending his horses.

"Woodrow Overholster, owner, blacksmith and general all-around hand," the man said as he stretched out a hand twice as big as Clay's.

Clay shook the man's hand and noticed his power and strength, and was glad he didn't try to show off. Instead, it was just a normal handshake. There was a certain gentleness to this giant of a man that most men would be inclined to overlook.

"Clay Brentwood, Texas Ranger," Clay said with a grin.

"And what brings a Texas Ranger to Oklahoma? A little out of your territory, aren't you?"

Clay grinned and looked at the hail piling up in the street. "Maybe, maybe not. I was told we had no boundaries as long as we were on the trail of somebody."

"That ah fact. You thinkin' this here outlaw you're after might be here in town?"

Clay shook his head, "I doubt it, but I'm bound ta look."

"Anybody I might have heard of?" the holster asked with a twinkle in his eye, hoping for the chance to see a Texas Ranger in action.

Clay thought for a moment. It might be a place ta start; holsters always seem ta know a lot about what was goin' on in their towns. "Hammershield, Aaron Hammershield. Ever hear of him?"

"Whooee, you got yourself a rattlesnake by the tail," the holster yelled, while slappin' his big hand on his leg. "I'm bettin' the sheriff would like to talk to you. He had a run-in with this Hammershield fella after he shot and killed Bill Small at the poker table; said he was cheatin'.

"Most everbody in town had known Bill for several years. He played cards maybe once ah week. Sometimes he won and sometimes he didn't, but nobody ever heard of him cheatin' afore. But this Hammershield, he had three men who witnessed the ordeal and swore the dead man had cheated by dealin' off the bottom."

"Associates of his, right?" Clay asked.

"Yes sir, that's what he called them, associates."

The noise stopped suddenly and they looked toward the door to see bright sunlight filling the sky.

Outside they looked off to the northeast and saw the black clouds and hailstorm moving toward Tulsa. The street was covered with about three inches ice balls.

"This sheriff have a name?" Clay asked.

"Sure does," the hostler said with a grin. "Russell Hogg. Ah good man. I think you two will get along just fine. His office is up the street bout two blocks on the other side, can't miss it. Just happened to see him go inside bout an hour ago. I reckon he should still be there."

When Clay walked into the sheriff's office, the sheriff was pinnin' up wanted posters and had his back to him. The sheriff never turned around but Clay saw him glance up at a mirror hanging nearby and take Clay's measure. When he finished, he turned around and held out his hand. "You must be Clay Brentwood, glad to meet you, I'm Russell Hogg, sheriff of Oklahoma City."

The sheriff knowin' his name took Clay by surprise. "Have we met?" Clay asked. "I think I would have remembered if we had."

The sheriff grinned from ear to ear and said, "No, son, we've never met. Your boss, Bill McDaniel and I, have been friends since boyhood. He sent me a telegram sayin' you might be driftin' this way, searching for an hombre by the name of Hammershield."

Clay looked at the sheriff and saw the gray hair sticking out from under his hat and the wrinkles in his face. Clay would put him somewhere in his fifties, the same as his boss.

Clay stuck out his hand and said, "You had me goin' there, for a minute."

By now it was coming up toward noontime and the sheriff suggested, since he'd missed breakfast, they go down to the diner and talk.

The diner was a fairly large room that would seat thirty people and was filled with several smells that immediately had Clay's taste buds jumpin' to attention. Fresh bread, apple, mixed with cinnamon, along with several other delicious odors that would make ah man want ta eat somethin' even if he wasn't hungry.

The sheriff picked a table where he could keep a lookout through the door.

They'd no more than sat down when a middle-aged woman came out of the kitchen and when she saw the sheriff, her eyes brightened up and a smile spread across her face as she sashayed up to the table. "I had a real good time last night, Russell," she said.

The sheriff's face turned the color of ah stomped on toe, all red and puffy. "Thank ya, Marcella. This here is Mister Clay Brentwood," he said changing the subject. "He's ah Texas Ranger, up here chasin' that Aaron Hammershield. You know, the one that shot and killed Bill Small; the one I couldn't haul off ta jail cause of his lyin' friends sayin' Bill had cheated at cards?"

Marcella turned her smile on Clay and he almost blushed from the look in her eyes. She stuck out her hand and said, "Glad to meet you Mister Brentwood. My name is Marcella Black. I own this here diner, and if you catch that lying no good piece of nothing that calls himself a man, and put him in jail, well… you just come by here and I'll fix you the best dinner you've had in a coon's age, and it will be on the house."

Clay stared at her and the only thing he could think of to say was, "Thank you, I'll do my best."

Their lunch consisted of beef stew that would melt in your mouth, fresh bread with whipped butter, black coffee, and for dessert, they had apple pie, covered with whipped cream. Not one word had been spoken while they ate.

Afterward, over more coffee, the sheriff gave Clay a lot of good information about the badlands, ending by saying, "It's a big place and not only could he be hidin' anywhere in there, he could move from place to place, making it even that much harder to catch him. Plus, there are several people who live there that, for a price, hide outlaws."

"If he's in there, I'll find him," Clay said with confidence.

"You might at that," the sheriff said, "but don't forget, he won't be alone. The way I hear it, he has some mean hombre's riding with him – killers, all of them."

"Yes, that might create ah problem or two," Clay said, leaving a dollar tip for the smiling owner of the diner, and said, "Can't ever remember eatin' stew that good, and nobody makes ah better apple pie than you."

"Careful now, ranger," the sheriff said with a chuckle as he winked at Marcella, "you'll be giving her the bighead."

"Oh, get on with you," she said giving the sheriff a shove. "And don't forget about tonight," she said as an afterthought.

As they walked toward the sheriff's office, Clay slapped the sheriff on the shoulder and said, "Sounds like you and Marcella are closer'n two peas in a pod."

The sheriff glanced back over his shoulder, then back at Clay. "She's a good woman," he said, nodding his head. "Her husband died a few years back. They had a small ranch just outside of town. Took a fall from a horse and landed on a sharp stick that punctured his heart. She still lives out there, but opened the diner to make a living. We've been seeing one another for about three months now."

"Well, I hope it all works out for the two of you. Don't know if runnin' ah ranch is any safer than sheriffin', but ta my notion it's ah lot more fun," Clay said, thinking about his own ranch.

"The truth is, probably more cowboys get killed because of bronc bustin' or getting' gored by some ole bad tempered bull, than by ah shootout. Of course, ah sheriff is always ah target by some drunk or hothead," he lamented.

The sheriff had a map of the Oklahoma Territory hanging on his wall, which Clay examined with great care, making a pencil sketch for his own use.

That evening, Clay got himself a nice hot bath and a shave, along with getting his clothes washed and ironed. He ate supper with the sheriff at the diner and once again ate like ah king – ah large steak, cooked just the way he liked it, fried potatoes covered with white gravy, green beans, fresh bread and creamy butter. And for dessert, he had a big slice of blueberry pie, covered with thick cream, and he savored every mouthful. He sure wouldn't get this kind of food out on the trail.

Back in his hotel room, Clay sat on his bed, studying the map he'd made. It took in a big area and he made mental notes for later, just in case the map got lost or destroyed.

-

The next morning, while Clay was saddlin' Midnight and puttin' the pack on the ap, the sheriff came by to see him off.

"Having breakfast before you go?" he asked as he walked up.

Clay looked over his shoulder and grinned. "Ate enough yesterday ta last for at least ah week. Had coffee at the hotel."

"Figured as much," he said. "Marcella got the notion you might be hungry by noontime and asked me to give you this," the sheriff said, handing Clay a package wrapped in brown paper.

"What's this?" Clay asked as he took the package.

"Couple of roast beef sandwiches and a piece of apple pie," the sheriff said, grinning from ear to ear.

Clay was a bit overwhelmed by the fact there were so many folks around that gave thought to other folks. He figured he been chasin' bad men too long.

Reaching into his pocket, Clay said, "Here let me give you some money for her and tell her that it was mighty thoughtful for her ta think of me."

The sheriff raised his palms up. "Don't you dare! You don't want to insult her, do ya?"

"No, I just..." Clay stammered.

"Well then just let me tell her how pleased you are, and let it go at that," the sheriff said in a stern voice.

"You do that, sheriff, you just do that, because I am mighty pleased, yes sir, mighty pleased indeed."

CHAPTER TWELVE

-

By the time Clay headed northeast for Tulsa, he figured he'd gotten a late start. "Must be around eight o'clock," he said to Midnight as he pulled out his pocket watch and looked down at it. "Ten past eight," he read aloud before giving the knob a few twists, and putting the watch back in his vest pocket. Clay looked at the location of the sun and nodded his head.

Few men in the west owned a watch but could look at the sun and be within a few minutes of the actual time. It was just one more way ta read sign.

He was less than a mile out when he heard what sounded like gunshots coming from behind him. He turned the black stallion around and sat looking back toward Oklahoma City, and sure enough, there were more gunshot sounds reverberating through the still air.

Intrigued, Clay rolled a smoke and lit it; then pulled his rifle from the boot and laid it across his lap.

The cigarette was nearly half gone before he saw two riders comin' his way, ridin' like the devil himself was after 'em. And maybe it was because from a long distance behind them came the report of rifle fire, followed by a puff of dust as the bullet landed wide.

The rider on Clay's left, lifted his arm and pointed a pistol in Clay's direction and in the next instant, a bullet whizzed past Clay's shoulder, followed by the report sounding in the air.

Without hesitation, Clay lifted his rifle and took careful aim and squeezed the trigger, and watched as the cowboy was knocked out of his saddle and went tumbling end over end across the dusty road.

The second cowboy turned his horse and began racing away toward a group of elm trees off to the west.

Clay raised his rifle and took aim, then all of a sudden, an idea popped into his mind and he chuckled. After putting his rifle back in its boot, he snubbed out his cigarette between his thumb and forefinger and threw the ashes to the wind. Next, he dropped the lead rope of the appaloosa and nudged Midnight with the sides of his boots, turning his head in the direction of the fleeing bandit.

"Let's go get 'em boy!" Clay yelled, and as if understanding what his master wanted, the black stallion leaped forward and stretched his long legs in pursuit.

When Midnight got close, the bandit looked over his shoulder, then pulled his pistol and took a shot in Clay's direction, but at the speed he was going and the rocking motion of the horse, his shot was wide.

Clay grinned and lifted his lariat and shook out a loop. Swinging the loop overhead he waited until he was close and just as the bandit lifted his pistol to take another shot, Clay let loose the loop and watched as it settled over the bandit's head. Jerking back on the rope, he wrapped it around the saddle horn and pulled the black stallion to a sliding stop.

The rope pulled taunt and Clay watched as the bandit was jerked off his saddle and landed on his back, the hard ground forcing a loud grunt to fill the air.

Stepping quickly from his saddle, Clay rushed over and pointed his hog-leg at a young man of no more than sixteen.

The young man's eyes grew big and he yelled, "Please don't shoot me, mister! It wasn't my idea to rob the bank, honest it wasn't. It was all Cryder's idea."

Clay was still starin' down at the young bank robber when sheriff, Russell Hogg and one other man rode up and swung down.

The sheriff walked over and looked down at the young bandit. "Well now, young Jimmy Shanks, is it? Never thought I'd ever have to hang a thief as young as you, but the law is the law, and bank robbing is a hanging offense."

Clay looked at the sheriff and said, "Can I talk to you in private?"

The sheriff turned to the other man and said, "Nate, keep an eye on this owlhoot and if he gives you any trouble, shoot him."

Nate pulled his six shooter and said, "Yes sir, sheriff, I'll do that."

Jimmy Shanks, the young bank robber, watched as Clay and the sheriff walked off just out of hearing distance. His heart was pounding so hard he figured he might die before they could string him up. He felt tears welling up in his eyes. He was scared. He didn't want to die. Why had he listened to Cryder? His mother had warned him, but he hadn't listened and now they were gonna hang him.

Out of hearing range, and with their backs to the young man, Clay spoke softly. "You really ain't gonna string him up, are ya?"

The sheriff grinned and said, "Naa, I just want to shake him up a bit. He's a good kid at heart – just got mixed up with a no good called, Cryder Johnston. Jimmy's father had a heart attack a couple of months ago while he was out plowing. They're going through a tough time, his ma and him. Like a lot of the sodbuster hereabouts, they're long on bills and short on money.

Clay rolled this information over and over in his mind before saying anything. Finally, he said, "How much is their place worth, you reckon?"

The sheriff had a puzzled look on his face and said, "I don't know for sure. They just homesteaded the place about four months ago so they're just getting started. I will say the place has potential. It's only fifty acres, but it's rich soil and has good water. I'd say, maybe five dollars an acre; say two hundred and hundred fifty dollars. Why do you ask?'

Clay said, "Got me an idea. Tell me what ya think."

After listening to Clay's idea, the sheriff shook his head and said, "If you don't beat all. Alright, I'll go along with it."

When they walked back, Jimmy was on his feet but still had the rope around him. Nate was standing a few feet away with his pistol pointed at the young bandit.

Clay walked over and took the rope off Jimmy and coiled it up and hung it over his saddle horn, then walked back and stood next to the sheriff.

"Son," the sheriff said, "you must have a guardian angel looking after you."

"Huh?" Jimmy said.

"Told the Texas Ranger here about your problems and he's got an idea; and if you go along with it, I think I can get the judge to consider not hanging you, or sending you to prison, but you'd be on parole for the next couple of years."

"What does that mean?" Jimmy asked.

"Parole means you won't go to jail or hang. It means you'll be free to work your place but you'll have to report to me every week and not break the law again. If you do, then I guess I'll have to hang you or put you in prison."

"Don't want either of those things, and as much as I'd like ta go along with this parole thing, I can't cause ma needs money ta live on until a crop comes in, and I don't know no other way ta get it for her."

"That's where the ranger comes in," the sheriff said. "He's offered to buy your place for ah hundred and fifty dollars. You and your ma can stay there, with you workin' the land."

Jimmy looked over at Clay. "Why would you do that? That's ah heap of money ta be puttin' out without knowin' me or what kind of farmer I'll make." Jimmy stated mater-of- factly. "And what makes you think I won't take the money and run?"

Clay looked the young man in the eyes and said, "My gut tells me you're not outlaw material, and I think given ah second chance, you'll turn out ta be ah solid citizen. Plus, I think you set store by your ma, right?"

Jimmy stared at Clay for what seemed a long time, then grinned and said, "Yes sir, I do. She's ah God fearin' woman, and I promise to work hard and keep my nose clean; yes sir, I will, if I can just get the chance."

"Well, you see that you do," Clay said and winked at the sheriff.

"Farmin' don't make a lot of money and I reckon you'll want half of the profits, bein' the owner and all. How will I get the money to you?" Jimmy asked.

Clay looked at him and said, "I've been givin' that some thought and here's what I come up with. You work hard and keep your nose clean for the next two years, and make that place pay for itself, along with provin' to the sheriff here, you've become ah solid citizen, then I'll sign the place over to you. You'll owe me nuthin' and the place will be yours, free and clear. But if you don't, you'll have every ranger in Texas breathin' down your neck."

"You mean that?" Jimmy asked, astonished by what the ranger said.

Clay looked at the young man and smiled and nodded his head. "I do."

The sheriff held up his hand. "Before any of that can happen, we need ta find out what the judge thinks of the idea, but I think he'll go along with it especially when you tell him about it bein' Cryder's idea."

All the joy went out of Jimmy's face. "You sayin' I got ta get up in front of everbody and tell that it was Cryder's idea and that I only went along cause me and ma was busted?"

Clay interjected. "Let us talk to the judge and maybe we can settle this in his chambers since you're only… How old are you, anyway?"

Jimmy stood up a little straighter. "I'll be sixteen in two months. I'm purty much full growed and I can do mans work."

Clay studied the young man who still had a streak of freckles across his nose, bright blue eyes and a strong jaw. His hands were big and looked strong. His father must have been a big man because Jimmy was near six feet tall, but still rail thin. Hard work with some beef and beans in his stomach and he should fill out just fine.

"How about readin' and writin'?" Clay asked.

"I can sign my name," Jimmy said, proudly.

Clay stood starin' at the sky for a moment, then turned to the sheriff. "I'd like ta add ah proviso."

"And what would that be?" the sheriff asked.

"In addition to the other things, Jimmy learns ta read and write and do his sums," Clay said with a grin. "He's gonna need all that ta run the farm proper like."

-

Back in Oklahoma City, after a long discussion with Clay and the sheriff, the judge held a private hearing in his chambers and agreed to the arrangement Clay had come up with. He also took a deposition, signed by Jimmy, about how the bank robbery was all Cryder's idea, after all, the money had been found in Cryder's saddlebags.

The judge felt himself a fair man, but had certain ideas about crimes and punishment and in his eyes, bank robbing was a capital offense, especially since he had money in the bank that had been robbed. Since Cryder had only been wounded, he gave him a choice –

hanging or go to prison. Cryder Johnston chose prison, which in this case would more than likely amount to the same end.

Ten years of hard labor in McAlester prison was practically the same thing as a death sentence. Very few lasted long enough to see the end of their term and those that did, were hard men that would not allow themselves to be broken. But even so, they weren't the same men that went in.

The prison was built in 1908 and designed after Leavenworth prison up in Kansas, which was also considered to be a hellhole. McAlester was situated on one thousand, five hundred and fifty-six acres and designed to be a maximum-security prison. When it first opened there were only fifty prisoners, but with so many outlaws coming west, the population was growing rapidly.

Clay went to an attorney in town and had him draw up a bill of sale for the Shank's farm, along with arrangements for the schoolteacher to give Jimmy private lessons on Sunday when he wasn't working. At the bank, he drew out a little extra for himself.

That night, Clay and the sheriff were both invited to supper so Clay could not only look over the land he had purchased, but to meet Jimmy's mother. She wanted to thank him and fix him a good meal before he started out again.

At somewhere near fifty, Emma Shank was still a strong woman who carried herself well. In her eyes and the lines beginning to form on her face, Clay could see hardship, even though she tried to mask it with her smile.

There were tears in her eyes as she held his hand, thanking him over and over for what he'd done.

CHAPTER THIRTEEN

-

As the blazin' sun crawled above the horizon with the promise of another scorching day, Clay rode north with a full stomach and a bag of the best biscuits he'd eaten in ah long while, stowed in his saddlebag, along with a jar of honey.

They were gonna be alright, Clay thought as he gave the black stallion his head and leaned back in the saddle, letting himself relax. Mister Shank must have had a good eye because the land he chose was some of the best in this part of the country. The soil was dark loam, rich with nutrients. They could grow most anything. And the grass was tall and green, which meant cattle or horses, would do well there, too. The creek that ran across the property was a stem off the Canadian, he believed, and ran into a small lake at the far end of the property so there would be plenty of water.

Between Mrs. Shank and her son Jimmy, the farm should prosper. He'd watched both of them carefully while he was there and got good vibes. There was no doubt that she was of strong stock and would hold up her end. Even though he still had some filln' out ta do, Jimmy had learned a site about farmin' and raisin' stock from his father.

Though he'd been embarrassed to admit what he'd done, Jimmy fessed up and took his reprimand from his ma, then relished in her forgiveness, promising to keep on the straight and narrow.

"It's nice ta be able ta help people who need helpin'," Clay said as he patted Midnight on the side of the neck.

The big horse responded by shaking his head up and down as though he'd understood every word.

Suddenly, the sun disappeared behind a huge black cloud that was dispersing a wall of rain with drops as big as Clay's thumb. Even though it was only water, the force of the raindrops stung his back and arms.

Touching his boots against Midnight's sides got an immediate response. The big horse had sensed the coming storm and was ready to run. And run he did, stretching his powerful legs to cover ground in a hurry, the ap not far behind.

Clay hoped he would find shelter soon. It was very possible the rain would or could turn to hail and a man didn't want to get caught out in a hailstorm. Without shelter, both he and his horses could get themselves killed.

The black stallion turned to his right and headed for a stand of elm trees off to the side of the trail.

The stand was thick and the branches overlapped each other enough to take the brunt of the rain. Clay stepped down and let the black stallion shake the rain off, then reached inside his saddlebag and pulled out his slicker, and put it on.

Stepping to a spot where he could see better, he watched the storm with a practiced eye. As far back as to when he'd been a youngster, he remembered storms like this one and knew they needed watchin'.

The wind was getting colder by the minute and the wind was now blowin' hard. Lookin' back over his shoulder, he wondered if he could find enough dry wood to light a fire and maybe make a pot of coffee.

After twenty minutes of lookin', he was about to give up when the rain and wind stopped all of a sudden like. Clay's head turned toward the west as he ran to the edge of the tree stand and looked toward the horizon. What he saw raised the hair on the back of his neck and he turned and ran back to his horse, grabbing the reins and urging them both deeper into the stand of trees.

He was close to the middle when he saw what he was looking for. The crevice didn't look very long or very deep, but it would have to do. The wind was now beginning to howl and it was getting harder to stand up. A quick look over his shoulder told him the tornado funnel would soon be upon them and he needed to be in that ditch before it reached the strand of trees.

Once they were in the ditch, Clay pulled Midnight's reins and pushed on his shoulder to get him to lie down in the bottom. Even as big and strong as he was, the black stallion was shaking, but did as his master wanted for he trusted him, as did the appaloosa.

Clay lay down between the horses with his arms across their necks and speaking in a calm tone. "It'll be alright. We just need ta stay layin' in this ditch till it passes over."

Above them, the trees were bending almost to the ground. Limbs were breaking off and bein' carried away. The roar of the wind was deafening and Clay felt the ground vibrate. There was nothin' else he could do but wait and hope it didn't suck them up into the funnel.

Tornados were not unusual in this part of the country. Back on his ranch, he'd lost three horses and several cows to tornados. He remembered seeing one of his horses runnin' hard to try and outrun the funnel, but was lifted off the ground and disappeared, never to be seen again.

Then, as suddenly as it came, it was gone, followed by heavy rain. As soon as it was clear, Clay stood up and helped his horses to stand, then hustled them both out of the crevice, and not a minute too soon. They had barely reached ground level when a wall of water roared over the sides, filling it to the brim.

That evening, Clay camped under the lea of an outcrop rock that not only helped keep the wind off his camp, but also helped hide his fire. Walking out away from the camp he looked back and smiled. You had to be practically in the camp to see it.

There was plenty of grass for the horses to eat and he enjoyed a meal of warmed up biscuits, honey and several pieces of bacon.

Clay heard a grunt and looked over his shoulder. Midnight was lying down just beyond the firelight and rolling in the grass before he called it a night. Neither of the horses were picketed, but Clay wasn't worried. They wouldn't go far and would come if he whistled. They would also alert him if danger come ah prowlin'.

Before turning in, Clay sat with his back against the outcrop rock and had a cigarette, while drinking the last of the coffee.

The sky was filled with excitement. Millions of stars were lighting up the night with their twinkling, and ever now and then, a shooting star would race across the sky.

As Clay climbed into his soogun, he wondered where Aaron Hammershield was and what he was doing?

Two more days and he would be in Tulsa and maybe pick up his trail.

CHAPTER FOURTEEN

-

Even though he didn't have it yet, Aaron Hammershield was thinking of ways to spend his share of the money his men were going to steal.

One of his thoughts was to drive the newly appointed Texas Ranger, Clay Brentwood, crazy looking for him – making him spend some of his money chasing false trails, while he lived high on the hog in Europe. He'd read books about the wealthy Dukes and Lords in Great Britain and their fancy castles and estates. Maybe he would buy himself a title and come back to New York and hobnob with the rich.

He poured himself a stiff drink and thought over his plan once more to make sure there were no flaws. He'd gone over the plans several times with his men and forced them to memorize the hand drawn map lying on the rough, plank board table.

They would reach Fort Smith, Arkansas by Saturday; spend the night hidden in a grove of trees along the Arkansas River, just outside of town until Sunday morning.

The way he had it planned, there would be no bank personnel, no opposition of any kind. The bank would be easy pickings. There were always two guards on duty and they rotated on twelve-hour shifts, but they would be pre-occupied by phase one of his plan and would easily be taken down. His men would be in and out and gone before anyone realized the bank had been robbed.

Then a hard ride up to Fayetteville, Arkansas for the second half of his plan – a change of horses and another hard ride back to their second hideout where he would count the money and give each man his share, then board a train for Kansas City and a new life.

Aaron Hammershield was a thinking man and, in his mind, a thinking man always came out on top. He had never actually been involved in the crimes he planned. For a cut of the bounty, there were always men who would do the dirty work for him. And… since he was the brains of the outfit, he naturally got the lion's share.

He walked outside and lit a cigar, blowing a smoke ring into the night air. The sky was filled with stars and every now and then Hammershield watched as a shooting star made its way across the sky. He'd heard that was a sign of good luck.

"Sure is ah purty night, ain't it, boss?"

Hammershield whirled and at the same time reached for the thirty-eight-caliber pistol hanging just inside his coat. When he saw who it was he released his grip on the gun.

"Don't you ever sleep?" he asked of the man standing a few feet away, grinning like a young boy who had just gotten away with a prank.

"Might ask the same thing of you. Reckon you just happen ta be up and about at the same time as I have the watch," Charlie Coots said.

Hammershield was about to ask how things were with the men when they heard two men yelling at each other.

"You cheated me! You dealt off the bottom, you no good theivin'…"

"I beat you fair and square! You just ain't no hand at poker, and that's the truth of it."

"So, you say, but I don't believe you and I ain't payin' you my share of the money when we get it!"

"You lowdown back peddlin' snake. You bet that money fair and square and you'll pay up or I swear…"

Both, Aaron Hammershield and Charlie Coots started to run toward the two men and had taken only a few steps when they heard the explosions – two pistols fired almost simultaneously. The roar filled the night air with two small puffs of smoke drifting lazily into the night sky.

When they got there, Clovis Sanchez was sitting on the ground holding his stomach. Blood was running between his fingers and staining the front of his shirt and pants. In the moonlight, his face seemed pale and his eyes were beginning to glaze over.

Hammershield looked down at him and knew the half French, half Mexican outlaw would be dead within a matter minutes, and it would be a painful death; gut shots always were.

Hammershield turned his head and looked down at Harley Bozeman. Harley was staring with vacant eyes at the sky. He was not wearing a shirt, but had on suspenders to hold up his pants. A small hole in the front of his chest right over the heart was oozing blood. He was dead.

By now, the other men had filed out from the two cabins where they'd been sleeping. To the man, they had pistols in their hands.

One of the men looked down at Sanchez and asked, "What happened?"

Sanchez looked up at him and said, "We were playing poker and Harley was having a streak of bad luck and that last hand, he bet all the money he would get from our next job. He lost, and then got mad – said I had cheated him – dealt off the bottom of the deck."

He looked up at Hammershield and said, "Senor, I have never cheated at cards in my life. I don't even know how to deal from the bottom of the deck. I..."

Sanchez's eyes got big and pain showed on his face as he took a last gasp of air and fell backward, dead.

Aaron Hammershield turned and looked at the other outlaws in his gang. His face showed no remorse or feelings of any kind. "Get some shovels and bury these two idiots. And let this be a lesson to all of you. Don't bet more than you can afford to lose."

With that, he turned and walked back to his own cabin. Inside, he poured whiskey into a tin cup and sipped it slowly. The death of these two men would not endanger his plans. Besides, Clyde Millsap would be there, and he would take up the slack. With the two of them gone, it meant a larger cut for each of the men and they would like that.

As for the two dead outlaws, they meant nothing to him, just two men who did his bidding and made him money. They were replaceable, as any of them were.

Tomorrow morning, they would head for Fort Smith.

Hammershield finished off his cup of whiskey and stood up. Outside, he could hear the men grumbling about digging a grave. They would bury them both in the same hole, and there would be no marker to show where they'd been planted. Like many men who went west, they would disappear and never be seen or heard of again.

Hammershield headed for his cot. Charlie Coots would see that the bodies were buried and the hole covered over leaving no signs of a grave ever being there. Charlie was a good choice as second in command. He was a tall, rawboned man from Mississippi who was tough and loyal – and the other outlaws respected him. Other than that, he knew little about the man, but what else did he need to know?

As for the Indian called, Kiowa, his only loyalty was to himself, but he was a good man to have in a fight and the men depended on him.

What he did with his share of the money, no one seemed to know. He didn't chase the whores, drink or smoke. Sometimes after a job, he would disappear for days at a time, then show up like he'd never been gone, wanting to know about the next job?

CHAPTER FIFTEEN

-

In spite of certain adversities, Loralie Benson already had a poke started. The first day she landed on ah spur that ran off of the Canadian, in the lower part of Colorado, she found a few nuggets; not big, but big enough to put in the leather bag she'd brought with her for that purpose.

The problem she was facing was not finding gold; it was the men who hadn't seen a woman in some time. Oh sure, once in a while, a miner would have a woman with him, but you could bet he wasn't sharin' her.

Sometimes a miner would go months without seein' a woman, and then it was probably a squaw. There just wasn't that many white women out here, yet. Someday they would come, but it would be awhile longer and then it would be married women who came with their husbands and family – nesters, they were called, or ladies of the night who worked the camps.

So, if a white woman showed herself out here, alone, it was news, and it spread like wildfire. For the most part, as long as a miner stayed sober, the women had nothing to fear; but a drunken man out here, no matter who he was, was not to be trusted to be a gentleman.

The first two days, their gawking amused Loralie. They would come down close to where she was standing knee deep in the water, washing river bottom around in her pan in hopes of seeing a nugget or two. There might be two or three of them, standing with their hats in their hands, just starin' and grinnin' at her. They never said anything, just gawked like they'd never seen a woman before.

The fact was, Loralie Benson was not just a plain lookin' woman. She was a handsome piece of female flesh that had a smile that made the men go weak in the knees and long red hair that glistened in the sun.

On the third day it happened. She had just climbed into her tent to get some much-needed rest. She was bone weary tired and her back hurt somethin' awful from standin' bent over all day, pannin' for the elusive gold nuggets. The moon was bright and a cool breeze was coming across the water.

She'd just pulled the blanket up over her when he rushed in and jumped on top of her, trying to kiss her. His breath reeked of whiskey and his beard scratched her face.

"Jest hold on, honey, this won't take long. I ain't seen no woman, especially one as purty as you in ah coon's age."

When he pulled the blanket off her to expose her naked body, he gasped and that slight hesitation gave Loralie the opening she was looking for. With her legs free, she drove her knee upward into the man's groin and heard him scream.

Then with both arms, she shoved him backwards and he went staggering out of the tent, bent over, holding his crotch and moanin' somethin' awful.

Taking her time, she pulled on her britches and shirt, then walked outside, barefoot. When the miner looked up at her, his eyes went wide. She was pointing a thirty-two-caliber pistol at his head.

"Oh please, ma'am, I didn't mean no harm. Please don't shoot me. It was the whiskey made me do it. If'n you don't shoot me, I promise ta bring you a bag of nuggets worth somewheres in the neighborhood of five hundred dollars and we can call the whole thing square. What'ya say?"

Loralie looked at him and shook her head. He looked so pathetic and scared that she almost laughed. Instead, she walked over and stared him right in the face, etching his face into her brain. "What's yer name?" she asked, pushing the barrel of the pistol against his throat.

The man swallowed and his Adams apple bobbed up and down. "Tom Dewmeyer, he said with a whisper.

"Well now, Tom Dewmeyer, you hightail it back ta where you come from and you tell the others that Loralie Benson from Cinch Mountain, Kentucky don't truck with men folks who come, plannin' on takin' advantage jest cause she's ah woman alone. I got me ah pistol and ah Winchester rifle, and I can shoot the eye out of ah squirrel at a hundred paces, on ah dark night. And in all my whole born put togethers, I ain't never lost ah wrestlin' match with ah man if'n I didn't want ta."

Tom Dewmeyer just stared and nodded his head up and down. "Yes ma'am, I'll do just that," he said.

Loralie stepped back and looked him straight in the eye and said, "And jest so's you'll know, I got six brothers, all fightin' men who take great store by their little sister. So, if'n anything should happen ta me…"

She let the last part trail off, letting the meaning sink in.

"Yes ma'am, I surely will spread the news and once again, my apologies for disturbin' yer sleep. Now, about that gold I promised, I'll come by tomorrow and…"

Loralie held up her hand. "You keep yer gold. You worked fer it and it belongs ta you. I'll get my own nuggets. You jest keep in mind, ah woman ain't just a thing ta be treated like property. You want ta get yer satisfaction, you treat 'em right. Be gentle-like; talk sweet and bring 'em presents. And talk to 'em like they was real people, cause they are!"

"Yes ma'am, yes ma'am, I'll remember that, for sure. Yes, ma'am I will."

"Well see that you do. Now git afore I change my mind and shoot ya where ya won't do no woman no harm anymore."

Still holding himself, but moving as fast as he could, Tom Dewmeyer disappeared into the trees, and shortly thereafter, she heard hoof beats falling away in the distance.

Back in her tent, she laid thinking. Hopefully, Tom Dewmeyer would spread the word and they would not bother her again. Even so, she couldn't stay here. There was only so much gold to go around in any given spot. Plus, two or more drunken miners might take it upon themselves ta pay her ah visit and she wasn't lookin' forward ta no killin'.

Somewhere in the back of her mind she resolved, her next pannin' site would be far removed from any other gold seekers. If there were no men around, she wouldn't have ta worry about bein' attacked, and possibly wind up shootin' somebody or at least breakin' some bones. As far as attacks go, there would always be bears, wolves and such; even Indians, but that was ta be expected. She just didn't want ta hurt no fellers just cause they was lonely, if she didn't have to.

She stared through the open flap of the tent and marveled at the size of the moon sitting just on top of the trees on the far side of the stream. She felt like she could climb one of those trees and reach up and touch it. A shiver ran through her as she wondered what she would have done if it had been that Texas Ranger, Clay Brentwood, who had come into her tent?

"Well, in the first place, he wouldn't have been drunk and tried ta force himself on you," she told herself. "He would have been a gentleman." She knew that by the way he'd been back on the trail.

She chuckled. "It would have been him that would have ta worry about her, not the other way around."

She felt a shiver run through her as she snuggled under her blanket and closed her eyes, wondering if they would ever see one another again?

CHAPTER SIXTEEN

-

The sun was past its zenith when Clay topped over a hill and looked out across the broad, green rolling hills. Except for a few patches of brown here and there from the lack of rain, the grass was mostly green. The trees were tall and filled out and a cool breeze wandered lazily across the land, with sudden gusts now and then. The sun glistened off the water of a broad river in the far distance

Situated along the Arkansas River in the foothills of the Ozark Mountains in the northeast part of Oklahoma, Tulsa was considered, at that time, to be the largest inland port in the country.

Tulsa had been originally settled by a band of Lachapoka Indians, which was part of the Creek Indian tribe. They called it, *Tallasi*, which meant, Old Town.

Then the white men came and settled here; changed the name to Tulsa and before long became an incorporated city. Today, Tulsa was a growing town with a bright future ahead of it.

Clay Brentwood reined in at the top of the knoll and stepped down to give the horses a breather while he stood looking over the town. He took off his hat and wiped his brow and the inside band of his hat. During this time of year, Oklahoma was hot and humid. He rolled a smoke, and then scratched the lucifer against the leg of his denim pants. Cupping the flame in his hands, he lit his cigarette, then dropped the matchstick on the ground and crushed it into the dirt. He wasn't about to start a fire.

Tulsa was bigger and busier than he expected it to be. He wondered if he would finally catch up with Aaron Hammershield here at the edge of the badlands?

No matter what the evidence back in Ardmore had pointed to, his gut told him he was still on the right track. Hammershield had tried to trick him into going to Denver, but he hadn't taken the bait. The man was nearby, he knew it; he could feel it.

Midnight snorted and shook his head, which told Clay the black stallion was ready to move on.

Stepping into the stirrup, he swung his leg over the saddle and settled in, giving his horse his head. Looking over his shoulder, the appaloosa was not far behind.

Less than an hour later, Clay stopped in front of the sign that read, Sheriff's Office, then stepped down and dropped the reins to the ground. By now, the appaloosa needed no lead rope because she stayed close to the black stallion.

As Clay stepped onto the wooden walkway in front of the sheriff's office, a young woman of about twenty, wearing a wide bottomed, flowery dress and sunbonnet tied under her chin, called to him. "Hey, Mister. You forgot to tie up your horses."

Clay turned in her direction and looked at her. The woman was plain looking with no outstanding features, except for a slight protrusion of her front teeth. He smiled and touched two fingers to the brim of his hat.

"No ma'am, I didn't forget," he said as he opened the door of the sheriff's office and stepped inside, leaving her standing there with her mouth open but nothing coming out.

The sheriff's office was a large room that consisted of three desks with wooden chairs, a potbellied stove, a large, wooden file cabinet, a locked gun rack that held several rifles, two shotguns and several handguns. The place was messy and smelled of stale food and cigar smoke.

The sheriff's desk sat away from the other two and on a raised platform so whoever sat at the desk could look out through the large picture window facing the street.

Behind the desk sat a walrus of a man with a handlebar moustache, dressed in a black suit with a star pinned on the lapel of his jacket. The man looked to be somewhere in the vicinity of three hundred pounds and stood well over six feet.

A sign on his desk, read, Wallingford T. Billingsley, Sheriff.

Hefting himself out of his chair, Sheriff Billingsley stood up and stared hard at the man standing in front of him. The man's clothes were dusty, indicating he'd just come into town after a long ride. Sheriff Billingsley took notice of the Ranger's badge pinned on the man's shirt. A Texas Ranger usually meant trouble and he didn't like trouble. In fact, he didn't like violence of any kind. That's why he had two deputies to do the dirty work.

He was an administrator, plain and simple.

"Something I can do for you, Ranger?" he said, putting inference on the word, Ranger.

The hackles on the back of Clay's neck stood on end and he took an instant dislike to the head of Tulsa's law enforcement. "I'm lookin' for a man who might be here in town or maybe passed through. Hopin' you might shed some light on him."

Sheriff Billingsley dropped back into his chair and took up his cigar, blowing smoke in Clay's direction. "And just who might this unsavory character be?" he asked. That he was already bored with the conversation was evident by the look on his face.

Clay's first instinct was to turn and leave. The man was a pompous ass and would more than likely be of no help, but… he needed information and possibly the man who called himself sheriff, could supply it if he was so inclined. "His name is Hammershield, Aaron Hammershield."

The sheriff sat up a little straighter and his face became serious. After tapping his cigar ash into a cup sitting on his desk, he asked, "And just what makes you think Mister Hammershield is anything but an upright citizen?"

"We must be talkin' bout two different men," Clay said. "The Aaron Hammershield I know is ah wanted criminal, and leader of a gang of bank robbin', cattle thievin', murderin' cutthroats."

"Then we are indeed talking about two different men with the same name. We have no one in Tulsa who fits that description. The Aaron Hammershield I know donates money to the church and school. His only vice that I know of, is enjoying a bit of poker from time to time, which in my books is not a sin, nor is it against the law."

The sheriff leaned back in his chair and blew another cloud of cigar smoke in Clay's direction.

"Anything else, Ranger?" He asked after a moment.

Clay knew he would get nothin' more from this man and rather than havin' ah shoutin' match about the merits of Aaron Hammershield, Clay decided to try a different venue. "No, I reckon not, sheriff. You've told me what I needed to know."

And with that, Clay walked out of the door, leaving the sheriff with a curious look on his face, wondering what information he'd given the ranger.

Outside, he stepped into the street and called to the big stallion, "Com'on, Midnight." He was in the mood to walk to the livery stable and knew both of the horses would follow.

People stopped and stared as the black stallion kept in step with his master, his chin over Clay's shoulder. The appaloosa trailed along, keeping pace with the both of them.

The holster at the livery stable grinned and spit a brown glob of tobacco juice into the dirt as Clay and his two horses walked up and stopped in front of him.

"I'll swan, I ain't never seen the like, mister. Them two horse sure take ah fancy to you, don't they? You train 'em to do that?"

Clay reached up and patted Midnight on the side of his face and said, "No, we're just good friends, that's all."

The holster shook his head and spit another stream of tobacco juice into the dirt. "Gonna be here long, Ranger?" he asked, noticing the badge for the first time.

"Not sure. Huntin' for ah man. If he's here I might be around for ah couple of days; if not I'll more than likely light ah shuck come mornin'. How much for the horses?"

The hostler grinned. "Do you want the regular care or do you want the full treatment which comes with groomin, rub down, grain, hay and ready for hard travelin'?"

"What's the difference in price?" Clay asked with a grin.

The hostler spit more brown tobacco juice into the dusty street, rubbed his jaw and said, "Four bits ah piece for regular and one dollar each for the works."

Two dollars was expensive, but Clay believed the old man would do what he said and the horses were in need of a good groomin'. Reachin' into his pocket, Clay pulled out two silver dollars and handed them to the hostler. "I reckon you talked me into the full treatment. You treat 'em good now, you hear."

The old man was grinnin' from ear to ear. "Yes sir, Mister Ranger. I'll see to it personal. Name's Caleb in case you're interested. You ask anybody, they'll tell ya, Caleb is the best anywhere's around here."

"That's fine, Caleb. I know you'll take good care of my friends here. My name's Clay Brentwood and I'll see you in the mornin'."

Clay walked down the sidewalk, glancing into the open doors of the various saloons, hopin' to see Aaron Hammershield sittin' at a poker table, but it was early and none of the saloons had much action yet. He was tempted to go in and talk to the bartenders since they knew pretty much everything that went on in town, but he was dirty and needed a bath; plus, he knew he needed to eat something before hittin' the bars for they would expect him to at least buy a beer if he wanted information.

A large sign up ahead read, Tulsa Hotel and when Clay walked in, his saddlebags over his left shoulder and his rifle hanging loosely in his right hand, several people stopped what they were doing and stared at him.

A tall, skinny man of about forty, in a white shirt and black vest, motioned him over to the counter. He had a look of concern on his face. "I know you're a Texas Ranger and all, but there are no guns allowed inside the city limits. Sheriff Billingsley sets store by that law and has instructed his deputies to arrest anyone carrying a gun," he said, his eyes looking toward the Winchester in Clay's hand.

"Well then," Clay said, smiling broadly, "I reckon you'd best rent me ah room in ah big hurry so's I have a place ta put my rifle so it won't do nobody no harm."

"That law also includes pistols," the clerk said, indicating Clay's big forty-four hanging on his hip.

"I thank you for that information. Now, how about that room? And I would also like to know if this fair city has a laundry and a bathhouse?"

The clerk grinned and said, "Yes sir. We have both attached to the hotel. I'll send someone to your room to collect the clothing you want laundered and direct you to the baths. We're only a small town at present, but we're growing every day. Placing a key on the counter, he said, "Room 106, on the first floor. I think you'll find it to your liking. That'll be one dollar."

Clay paid the clerk and was headed down the hallway when a thought crossed his mind and he turned around and went back to the counter. "Excuse me, ah… I'm sorry but I don't know your name?"

"Clarence. Clarence Baumgartner," the clerk said with a smile. "And what else can I do for you, Mister Brentwood?" he asked, looking down at the register.

"You wouldn't happen ta have a man stayin' here by the name of Aaron Hammershield, would you?"

Clarence smiled and said, "No, Mister Hammershield left us several days ago."

Clay nodded his head. "He didn't happen to say where he was headed, did he?"

"No sir. Mister Hammershield kept mostly to himself."

Clay laid another dollar on the counter. "Thanks."

After a long soak, a shave and dressed in clean clothes, Clay ate dinner at the hotel restaurant before heading for the saloons. He was dressed in the suit he'd had cleaned and as usual, the big forty-four was hanging from his hip, mostly covered by the length of his jacket. His badge was pinned to his shirt, also hidden by his jacket. He figured he might get more information if they didn't know who he was.

The first saloon he went into had only a few customers. Two men were standing at the bar discussing business. A cowboy was sitting at a table, talking to one of the girls who worked there, and in the back of the room four men were playing poker.

Clay walked up to the bar and ordered a beer and when the bartender brought it to him, he asked, "Lookin' for a man to play poker with by the name of Hammershield. You happen to know where I might find him?"

The bartender shook his head. "Not in here, mister. When Mister Hammershield is in town, you can usually find him over at the Lucky Seven. Not enough action for him here. I don't think he's in town right now. Heard he was here a few days back, though. Maybe you should check with Will Baker, he's the night barman over at the Seven."

Clay laid a dollar on the bar, left the glass of warm beer sittin' on the counter, and said, "Thanks."

The Lucky Seven had the look and smell of money to it. Everything inside was of a lavish nature – a huge chandelier twinkled as it reflected the light coming from forty candle lit lamps. The bar was an easy fifty feet long and had a brass spittoon next to the foot rail about every ten feet. At the far end of the room there was a stage with seventy-five chairs in front of it. Along the right wall was a piano and the man who was playing had obviously studied somewhere. He was good. The five poker tables were scattered in among the other tables that filled the room. Three of them were doing a thriving business.

Clay walked over and laid his hands on the bar. When the bartender approached, he asked, "You have any cold beer?"

"Only for those who ask for it. Most of the cowboys drink it at room temperature," he said with frankness.

"Then, I'd like a cold beer," Clay said, "and I'd like a word or two with Will Baker if he's around."

The bartender looked at him curiously and said, "I'm William Baker. What is it you want to talk about?"

"Nothin' earthshakin'," Clay said. "First things first, my throat is kinda dry."

William Baker brought him a mug of cold beer and stood waiting while Clay took a long pull.

"Ahh, now that's good," Clay said, sitting the mug down on the bar.

"Cool beer is ten cents. Information costs five dollars," William Baker said.

Clay looked at him and what he saw impressed him. The man was just under six feet tall, and well built. His face was handsome in a rugged sort of way. He looked as though he might have spent some time in the ring, and by the way he carried himself, a man who bucked him would have his hands full – yet there was an intelligence about him.

Clay laid six dollars on the bar and said, "Like I said, nothin' earthshakin'. I'm lookin' for a man by the name of Aaron Hammershield. I was told by the bartender across the street that he plays poker here when he's in town."

"Hammershield. Yeah, I know him. He ah friend of yours?" Will asked.

Clay decided to lay his cards on the table, so to speak, and tell it like it was, hoping he was making the right decision. "Not exactly," Clay said, pulling back the lapel of his coat and showing the bartender his badge. "Texas Ranger. I got paper on the man and I aim to take him into custody."

"Kinda thought there was something underhanded about him," the bartender said, shaking his head. "He always has some unsavory dregs hanging around close by. He was in here a few days back, but just passing through, he said."

"He didn't happen ta mention where he was goin', did he?" Clay asked, hoping for more information.

"No, he didn't say anything to me, but..." The bartender raised his hand. "Ah fella came through here yesterday and had a few drinks. Got talkative as most of them do when they're drinking. Happened to over hear him telling one of the men he was drinking with that he was on his way to meet up with Hammershield."

Clay sipped on his beer, trying not to show his excitement, while waiting patiently for the bartender to finish.

"Let's see, where was it he said he was headed for?"

Clay laid another five dollars on the bar and nudged it in the direction of the bar tender.

William Baker eyed the money and raised his eyebrows. "Oh yeah, now I remember. He said he was on his way to Fort Smith, Arkansas. Told the man something big was about to go down and he was to be a part of it. Heard him say he had to be there no later than Saturday evening."

Clay felt excitement well up inside him. He was finally gettiin' ah break.

"This fella didn't happen ta be a big man; walked with a swagger and went by the name of Clyde?"

The bartender thought for a moment, then said, "Now that I think about it, when he came in, that fella he was drinking with called him, Clyde, Clyde Millsap, or something like that."

Clay finished off his beer and stuck out his hand. "Thank you. You've been more help than you can imagine."

Back in his hotel room, Clay spent time cleaning his pistol and his rifle. He could feel a showdown comin' and he wanted to be ready. The last thing he needed was one of his weapons ta not work when he needed it. Things like that is what got ah man killed.

Now, what would Hammershield be doin' in Fort Smith, Arkansas? Wasn't that where the hangin' judge, Judge Isaac Parker, held jurisdiction, he wondered? Clay wasn't sure about the total, but he would bet Judge Parker had hanged more than a hundred men. It made no sense to pull a job there, unless Aaron Hammershield was tryin' ta show off. More of that egomania that Hammershield was so full of.

Hammershield is gonna pull ah heist of some kind, in Fort Smith, Arkansas, but what? Clay lay on his bed, staring at the ceiling, allowing his mind to wander. Suddenly, he swung his legs over the side of the bed and sat up.

What if there was a payroll comin' through Fort Smith? Or there was a lot of money in the bank for some reason. Sunday mornin' would be the perfect time ta pull it off – everbody would be in church. The town would be practically empty.

What Hammershield's plan was, he wasn't sure, but he'd bet the man was plannin' ah robbery right under Judge Parker's nose. How he would do it and how they would get away he didn't know, but his gut told him he was right.

Standing up, Clay strapped on his gun and grabbed his hat. Right now, he needed to go down to the train depot where the telegraph office was located and get a telegram off to the sheriff at Fort Smith, telling him of his suspicions.

As Clay stepped out of the hotel, two men, one on each side of him were standing there with pistols drawn and pointing them at him. Deputy badges were pinned on their vest fronts.

"You boys have a problem?" Clay asked in a calm voice?

The one on Clay's left; a large man with the face of a bulldog, indicated with his pistol. "You're under arrest. We don't allow firearms inside the city limits. Now unbuckle your pistol belt and let it drop."

Clay could see the sheriff's mind behind this; these boys didn't look like they could come up with an idea between 'em.

Slowly, Clay opened his jacket and nodded toward his own badge. "Sorry, gentlemen, but I'm a Texas Ranger, a lawman just the same as you are, and I don't give my gun to anyone."

"Thet don't cut no ice with us. You ain't in Texas now, boy. You're in Tulsa, Oklahoma and we got us a law thet says, no guns are allowed inside the city limits. Now, are you gonna shuck your gun, or do we have ta take it from you?" the deputy on Clay's right asked.

Clay looked over at him and saw a man with blood in his eyes. He was one of those men who thought wearin' ah badge made him bad.

Clay figured pullin' iron would be a fifty-fifty proposition. He knew he could get at least one of them for sure, but he didn't particularly like killin' a man just because he was stupid.

Without a word, and before either of them could react, Clay reached out with both hands and grabbed the deputies by the wrists holding their pistols, and jerked.

Both men were yanked forward and slammed their faces into one another.

Unexpectedly jerked off their feet caused both men to pull the trigger on their pistols and resulted in them shooting each other in the thigh.

Both men dropped their guns and grabbed their legs, screaming at the top of their lungs.

The deputy on Clay's right looked at him and said, "You done shot us!"

Clay reached down and picked up their guns and said, "I didn't shoot anybody. You shot each other."

Clay turned and started walking toward the train depot. Along the way, he tossed one of the pistols on the roof of the mercantile store, and the other one, on the roof of a ladies store, both closed for the night.

Clay finished sending his telegram and was about to head back to the hotel. He would need a good night's sleep. It would be hard riding for the next two and a half days to get to Fort Smith in time to help defuse whatever plans Hammershield had in mind.

As he turned toward the door, it was suddenly filled with a man carrying a shotgun.

"Evenin', Sheriff. Didn't know you made night rounds," Clay said with a wide grin.

The telegraph operator disappeared behind the counter as Sheriff Billingsley walked into the office.

"Clay Brentwood, I'm placing you under arrest for violating the no gun ordinance and for shooting both of my deputies," Billingsley said in a gruff voice."

"In the first place," Clay said, tired of these stupid people. "I didn't shoot anybody. They shot each other. And second, and hear me loud and clear, I'm an officer of the law, a Texas Ranger and I have no jurisdiction limitations, and I surrender my guns to no one. So, unless you plan on usin' that scattergun, you'd best step aside and let me go on about my business. You do that and I'll be out of here tomorrow mornin'."

Sheriff Billingsley stared at Clay, uncertain what to do. He wasn't used to opposition.

"On the other hand," Clay continued, "if you think you've got me dead to rights and plan on squeezin' that trigger, before I go down, I'm gonna put a bullet dead center in your heart."

Clay could see doubt in the sheriff's eyes, and sweat popping out on his forehead.

"Like I said," Clay continued, "you can try your luck and maybe you'll get me, but even if you do, you're gonna end up in the local graveyard, too."

Clay stepped back; his feet spread slightly apart, his hand hovering over the butt of his pistol. He looked the sheriff straight in the eyes and said, "Well sheriff, what's it gonna be?"

Clay saw fear in the man's eyes and sweat running down his face and drippin' off his chin. It was a tense moment where anything could happen because the sheriff's hand was beginning to shake and he might pull the trigger out of sheer panic.

Finally, the sheriff lowered the shotgun and said, "You just make sure you're out of town come sunrise."

Clay touched two fingers to the brim of his hat and walked out the door, showing his backside to the Tulsa lawman, figuring he wouldn't shoot him in the back, especially in front of the telegraph operator, who had by now stood up and moved to the side of the room, eyes wide, not wanting to miss anything. This would be a story worth telling.

When the ranger had gone, the sheriff turned toward the telegraph operator and said, "You mention even one word of what you saw and I'll see that you not only lose your job but get run out of town on ah rail. You understand me?"

The telegraph operator shrank back behind the counter and said, "Why sheriff, I don't know what you're talking about. I haven't seen or heard anything."

The sheriff harrumphed and walked out the door.

CHAPTER SEVENTEEN

-

The next morning Clay was in the dining room just as it was opening up, had an early breakfast, then rousted the holster out of bed and within minutes, was ridin' southeast, with some one hundred and twenty miles between him and Fort Smith, Arkansas starin' him in the face.

He had a hard ride ahead of him and there was no use wasting time. He could have taken the train, but that would have meant waiting an extra day at least, maybe longer because of the Indians who did not like the Iron Horse, as they called it, destroyed the tracks by dragging pieces of rail off to the side, causing long delays.

Repair crews were hard pressed to put together because they feared being attacked and maybe scalped or worse, diein'. The only crews, who could and would repair the tracks, were the Irish. The only problem was there were not many of them around, and the ones that were, were in jail for bein' drunk and disorderly, and for fightin'.

Clay had worked it out so he could eat up as much territory as possible without wearing out his horses. He would ride the black for two hours, take a short break while he gave them a blow and a little water – changed his saddle to the other horse and then ride two more hours. This way both horses would be able to go longer distances before he had to make camp.

Fate must have been smiling down on him because the weather turned cooler as dark gray clouds filled the sky, along with a cool breeze coming from the west.

The first day he figured he covered more than fifty miles and neither horse was worn down. Some water and grain and a good night's rest and they would be ready for another long day.

After a quick supper of bacon and beans, Clay sat with his back leaned against a tree and watched as both horses rolled in the grass before settling down for the night.

Neither of them was tethered. They might wander a bit, but not so far, he couldn't call them if he needed them in a hurry, nor far enough they couldn't alert him if someone or somethin' was getting close to the camp.

The next day was much like the day before, just miles and miles of nuthin' but miles and miles. The land was rolling hills filled with luscious green grass and clumps of trees. In the distance he saw mainly farms, but very few people, and those he did see were mostly farmers plowin' their fields.

There was no time to stop and talk. He had a job to do and he meant to be done with it. Aaron Hammershield had been a thorn in his side long enough. He wanted the man behind bars where he belonged, and then, hopefully he could finally go home and rebuild his ranch.

Somewhere in the back of his mind he wondered if that gal from Kentucky would like the life of a rancher's wife?

"Now where did that come from?" he asked himself, aware that they would more than likely never cross paths again.

Clay had basically followed the Arkansas River as it wound its way southeast, allowing him water and campsites. Like many other towns, Fort Smith also sat next to the river, just on the border between Oklahoma and Arkansas. At this time, Fort Smith was still in its growing period, which was not moving along as fast as the city fathers wanted it to because several businessmen had shied away. Many believed the town was in the middle of tornado alley and they were afraid of losing everything to mother nature.

Being a careful man, Clay swung north and crossed the river a few miles from town and continued on. He believed coming into Fort Smith from the northern side, to be the safe side without being spotted by Hammershield or his men.

The reason for this was plain. On the northern side of town there was no place to hide within two miles, while on the other three sides, there were stands of trees where they could wait to strike without being seen.

The sun was down and the moon was climbing into the cloudy sky when Clay eased up to the back door of the sheriff's office and tapped lightly.

The light inside went out and the back door opened only wide enough to shove the end of a double-barreled shotgun out just far enough to do a great deal of damage, but not far enough for a man to grab hold of.

"Speak your peace and it better be good or you're gonna gain weight. This shotgun is loaded with double ought buckshot and I can't miss," a gruff voice said from inside.

Clay had stepped back from the door and raised both hands in the air. "Texas Ranger, Clay Brentwood, the one who telegrammed Sheriff Kilgore about Hammershield and his gang."

CHAPTER EIGHTEEN

-

Aaron Hammershield was sitting with his back against a tree drinking coffee laced with whiskey and was in one of his better moods. Everything was going as planned except for the arrival of Clyde Millsap. But to be truthful, the man wasn't late, yet.

The thought had no more than passed through his brain when he heard hoof beats and a shout from just outside the camp. "Hello the camp... It's Clyde Millsap."

Charlie Coots looked over at Hammershield who nodded.

"Well come on in. Yer late and the boss is steamin'. We got better things ta do than sit around waitin' on an owl hoot like you," Charlie called out good-naturedly.

Clyde Millsap rode into the camp and looked around and when his eyes found Charlie, he said, "Charlie Coots, you no good cuss, I heard you'd met your maker."

"Just ah slight irritation to my right arm, and still a sight from my heart. I'll take care of your horse while you grab ah cup of coffee and then go have ah confab with the boss. He's waitin' fer ya over under that weepin' willer tree, yonder."

"Thanks," Clyde said as he handed the reins over to Charlie.

Clyde hunkered down on his haunches in front of Hammershield and sipped his coffee. "Got here soon as I could," he said between sips. "Had a bit of trouble with ah ranger back in Oklahoma City."

Hammershield's eyes lit up. "Did you say, Oklahoma City?"

"Yeah, said his name was Brentwood. He was askin' questions about you, so I butted in and tole him I didn't like rangers and challenged him to a shootout, but he turned yeller and backed down."

Hammershield looked at Clyde in disbelief. He had a hard time believing Clay would back down from the likes of Clyde Millsap, but held his thoughts.

"He backed down, did he?" Hammershield asked to see where this was going.

"Yup, right there in front of the whole saloon."

"And was that the end of it then?"

"No sir, not by ah long shot. Oh, he tried ta walk away, but I follered him out inta the street and challenged him with my fists. Of course, by now, near everbody in town was standin' there gawkin' at us and he didn't have no choice but ta try ta make a show of it."

"Are you saying you and this Brentwood went at it toe to toe?"

"Well not exactly. It weren't much of ah head banger. I'd hit him and he'd hit the ground. Then I'd haul him up and do it all over again," Clyde said trying to look big in front of Hammershield.

"But you didn't kill him, then?"

"No sir. Like I said, the whole town was standin there gawkin at us and it wouldn't ah looked good me beatin' him ta death. But he should be laid up for ah spell, so you got no worries about him buttin' his nose inta this caper."

Aaron Hammershield leaned back against the tree and studied Millsap. The man was a bruiser, there was no doubt about that, and fast with a gun, but Clay Brentwood was no slouch when it came to the manly art of fisticuffing, or pulling iron, and from the looks of Millsap's face, Brentwood got in a few licks of his own. Of course, he would have to rely on what Clyde said and hope for the best, but he would keep his eyes open.

Hammershield called them together and once again laid out his plan of attack, dictating what their jobs would be. The packhorse with the money would be the responsibility of Charlie and Clyde. They were to ride past a gypsy wagon headed west and toss the bags of money into the back as they went by. The others were to ride off in the opposite direction, distracting anyone who might try to follow.

After dropping off the money, Charlie and Clyde were to head for Fayetteville where they would all meet up for the second job.

The whole Fayetteville job would be theirs to split, all he wanted was the half million from today's take which, added to what he already had stashed away, would be enough for him to retire on.

Hammershield had previously made a deal with a gypsy fortuneteller to use her wagon. For fifty dollars she would ask no questions. Disguised as a gypsy, himself, they would transport the money several miles to the west, where he had another wagon stashed – one with a false bottom.

Once he got to the wagon with the false bottom, he would send her on her way and then change disguises. This time he would pose as a circuit preacher on his way to Denver, carrying several cases of bibles, with the money hidden in the false bottom.

It was perfect. He could not be connected to the crime because he would be nowhere near. If the men followed his plan to the letter, it would come off without a hitch and he would be five hundred thousand dollars richer. What happened in Fayetteville was no concern of his, but if they followed his plan, they should be able to split seventy-five thousand dollars.

Although he hadn't told anyone, this was to be his last job. He had four hundred eighty thousand dollars in a bank up in Wichita to add to the half million he would make today.

It had taken him five years and a lot of robberies to finally have enough to retire on.

After closing out the bank account in Wichita, he would change his name and maybe even grow a moustache or a beard. After a year or so touring Europe, he should be able to come back and buy a small spread in South Carolina and live the life of a gentleman.

"Alright, men," he said, "I suggest you turn in and get some rest. Tomorrow we clean out Fort Smith."

Most of the men were too keyed up to sleep, but knew they needed to rest. It wasn't just the robbery tomorrow; they had a hard ride to Fayetteville and a second robbery, then a hard ride back to their hideout without getting caught.

Each man crawled into his soogun and thought about what he was going to do with his share of the money.

One was going to go to Mexico and buy a small ranch, while another planned on going back to Wisconsin and setting himself up with a store of some kind.

It wasn't unusual for a man to go on the outlaw trail to try and make enough money so he could turn legitimate. Most never made enough to see their dreams come true, but they kept trying. The majority got themselves shot down during the robbery or captured and hung.

Of course, the others just wanted to get drunk and chase women until the money ran out, then go rob someone else. Some outlaws never changed, nor did they want to.

CHAPTER NINETEEN

Clay told the Fort Smith sheriff everything he knew and when he finished, he sat back and sipped on the cup of black coffee he'd been given.

Sheriff Bill Hancock stood up and paced the floor while he puffed on a cigar. Finally, he stopped directly in front of Clay. "What you've told me makes sense. There's a half a million-dollar payroll sittin' in the bank up the street. The Army isn't due in here to pick it up until Tuesday, so if a man was gonna rob the bank, Sunday would be a good time. Almost everbody in town will be at the church." The sheriff rubbed his jaw. "But you don't know how he plans on doin' it, or for sure that he's even gonna try?"

"That would be right," Clay said, "but I know Hammershield, or at least think I do and my gut tells me he's goin' after that payroll, and it's gonna be tomorrow durin' church time."

Clay watched as the sheriff began to pace, again. He was of medium height, maybe five foot nine and weighed about a hundred and sixty pounds in his stockin' feet. His dark brown hair was beginning to have streaks of gray along the temples. His skin was tan from bein' in the sun a lot and his eyes were always on the move. Clay liked this man. He was a thinkin' man, not prone ta goin' off halfcocked – and he seemed to have no fear in him.

Finally, the sheriff stopped and poured a cup of coffee for himself, then walked over to his desk and sat down. "Clay, is it?" he asked.

Clay nodded and waited for the sheriff to continue.

The sheriff sighed and asked, "Clay, do you have any ideas as to how he might go about getting into a safe that's guarded by six hard men?"

Clay thought for a moment. "The only thing I can tell you is – be ready for anything and everything. Aaron Hammershield hasn't evaded the law for as long as he has by bein' stupid. You can bet he's been here and knows how many guards you have and where they will be when he makes his play, and what he's gonna do to distract them."

"And you say he's never at the scene of the crime?"

Clay thought for a moment then said, "I can't say he won't be somewhere close by so he can keep an eye on things, but so far, nobody has ever actually seen him at the scene of the crime."

"Any ideas on how we should set things up?" Sheriff Hancock asked.

Clay grinned and said, "Well sir, now that you ask.

CHAPTER TWENTY

-

Sunday morning proved to be a beautiful day. The sun was bright in the sky and a gentle breeze eased its way down the main street of Fort Smith, Arkansas. If a man didn't know better he'd think this was the most peaceful town west of the Mississippi.

But Fort Smith was far from being peaceful. There were twenty-five deputies posted at strategic positions along both sides of the street, on tops of buildings and where they could see the rear of the bank. The six guards were still posted inside the bank with orders to stay inside, no matter what happened outside. They sat behind mattresses with thick pieces of hide stretched across them to help stop bullets if they came in shootin'.

At exactly nine-thirty, several cowboys rode into town from four directions, just as folks were makin' their way to the church at the far end of town.

As one of the deputies watched from the rooftop of a building, he saw two men ease up next to the side of the mercantile store window. One of them was carrying four sticks of dynamite tied together. A short fuse was stuck into one stick of the dynamite.

Two other cowboys, who had hidden their horses into the alley, strolled up in front of the bank and stood talkin' like this is what they did every day. One of them was carryin' a gunnysack.

All the deputies had been instructed to use their own judgment once the dance started.

At two minutes to ten, a cowboy came ridin' down the street real slow like. The church doors were open because of the heat and the organ music could be heard loud and clear. Just as the people began to sing, Rock of Ages, he lifted his hat and wiped his face on the sleeve of his shirt.

At that moment, one of the men in front of the bank pulled four sticks of dynamite from the gunnysack, while the other man struck a lucifer, then lit the fuse.

At exactly the same time, the men at the side of the mercantile store did the same thing.

When the fuses were lit, the men holding the dynamite raised their arms, ready to throw their packages through the windows of both the bank and the mercantile store.

When each man's arm reached the top and he was about to bring his arm forward, two gunshots echoed through the music-strewn air.

The dynamite exploded, killing all four men and knocking the man on the horse into the street. At that point all hell broke loose as deputies came from seemingly out of thin air; from the church, from the tops of buildings, from out of back doors, out of the livery stable, all armed and ready to fight.

When the bandits realized they were caught in a trap, they pulled iron and began to shoot at anything that moved, looking for an escape route.

Clay Brentwood had stationed himself down near the livery where he could see what went on. His only blind spot was the backside of the bank. He watched as the cowboy came riding down the street, and in the far distance behind him, he saw a gypsy wagon turn off and go toward the backside of town, on the same side as the back of the bank would be.

Midnight was saddled and ready to go. Clay turned and put his foot into the stirrup, then swung up and sat down easy on the saddle as he guided the big horse to a spot next to the side of a building not far from the bank and got down.

Peering around the side of the building he could see the gypsy wagon had stopped a short distance beyond the back door of the bank. The man driving the wagon looked like a gypsy, with his long black hair, dark skin and thick mustache, yet there was something familiar about him.

Clay eased back to his horse and took a pair of binoculars from his saddlebag, then went back and raised them to his eyes.

After only a moment, he lowered the glasses and grinned. "Hammershield, you sure are one devious son of a gun."

It had taken Clay only a moment to see through the disguise and know what the plan was.

He'd just put the binoculars back in his saddlebag when the air was filled with loud explosions and gunfire. Pulling his pistol, he ran back to the edge of the building and stepped around the corner to see what Hammershield was doing and almost got run over. When all hell broke loose, Hammershield jumped ship, and was driving the team as hard as he could to get away.

When Clay stepped out from behind the building, he found himself directly in the path of the escaping wagon. One of the horses slammed into him and knocked him backward to the ground. Getting up, he dropped his pistol into his holster, then sprinted for his horse.

Hammershield had a good lead, but the black stallion was well rested and ready to run.

Less than half a mile out of town, Clay saw Hammershield in the opening at the back of the wagon and he had a rifle in his hand.

Clay drew his forty-four and fired at the retreating wagon. He saw a piece of the canvas rip, close to Hammershield's head.

Hammershield ducked, then threw a hasty shot in Clay's direction that whistled past his shoulder.

Clay fired again and saw Hammershield disappear back inside the wagon.

Through the back of the wagon, Clay saw that Hammershield was back on the driver's seat, slapping the reins hard against the horses' backs, cursing them, yelling for them to run faster. What happened next was a major surprise.

The gypsy woman grabbed the reins, jerked them out of Hammershield's hands, then turned on her side and kicked Hammershield in the side with both feet, sending him flying in the air.

Aaron Hammershield landed hard and rolled over several times, but somehow came up on all fours and looked in the direction of Clay Brentwood.

Clay dropped his pistol back in his holster and pulled the black stallion to a halt. He stepped down and as he walked toward Hammershield, he said, "Aaron Hammershield, I arrest you for the crimes of murder, attempted murder, resistin' arrest and breakin' jail. I'm takin' you back ta Texas ta stand trial for the aforementioned charges against you. Are you comin' peaceful like, or am I gonna take you back face down over a saddle?"

The gypsy woman had stopped her wagon and turned it around and had just driven up as Clay made his speech. She looked at Clay and said, "He beat my horses and yelled curse words at them. I do not like."

Clay nodded toward the gypsy woman, and when he did, Hammershield grabbed for his pistol and took a quick shot, searing Clay's cheek.

Clay drew and fired. Hammershield's pistol flew from his hand, but the man was not ready to give up. He reached inside his coat and pulled out a hideout thirty-two caliber pistol and pointed it in Clay's direction. "You aren't taking me anywhere, ranger. It's you who is going home face down over the saddle."

There was a loud roar and Clay turned in time to see the gypsy woman pulling the trigger on an old sharps rifle – the impact knocking her back into the wagon.

Aaron Hammershield was hit in the back and the bullet from the big rifle, at that range drove itself all the way through and came out his chest.

Eyes wide, Hammershield tried to say something, but nothing came out but blood. It trickled over his lips, staining his shirt, then slowly, he fell face first into the dirt.

"He beat my horses, and he cursed them. They are good horses. They are my friends," the gypsy woman said as she climbed down from her wagon and walked over to where Hammershield lay. She looked at him for a moment, then spit on his dead body.

"He no hurt my horses no more," she said matter of factly, then turned and walked back to her wagon and climbed up on the seat.

"No ma'am, I don't reckon he will," Clay said, not knowin' what else ta say.

About then the sheriff and three deputies rode up. The sheriff looked down and asked, "That him?"

"That's him," Clay said with a sigh.

"What'ya shoot him with, ah canon?" one of the deputies asked.

Clay thought for a moment, then said, "Somethin' like that."

The sheriff looked back and forth between Clay and the gypsy woman, but said nothing until the gypsy woman turned her wagon and started on down the road. Looking at Clay he asked, "You just gonna let her drive off?"

Clay grinned and said, "Sure, why not? What's she gonna do, testify that she saw me kill Aaron Hammershield?"

CHAPTER TWENTY-ONE

-

Clyde Millsap was angry and figured he had a score ta settle with that uppity ranger, Clay Brentwood, and he wanted his due. Not only had the ranger whipped him in front of the whole town, back in Tulsa, where he could never show his face again thout shootin' somebody fer laughin' at him.

His second score ta settle with the ranger was fer messin' up the bank job, today, which had cost him ah site of moncy.

He and Charlie Coots had barely gotten away. If'n they hadn't been laggin' back, playin' it cautious, they would have been killt right along with the others.

Clyde Millsap wiped the sweat from his forehead with the back of his hand. His nerves were ragged and his arms were tired from holding the nine-pound Henry rifle against his shoulder. "Com'on, Mister Texas Ranger man. Come and meet yer maker," he said in the direction of the hotel restaurant where nearly the whole town was celebratin'.

Thanks to the Texas Ranger, Clay Brentwood, the people of Fort Smith had taken down the Hammershield gang and prevented a bank robbery that would have cost them more than fifty thousand dollars.

Clyde was tempted ta try and shoot through the window but his odds would be better if he waited until his target came out onto the sidewalk.

Bein' the coward he was, Clyde chose ta shoot the ranger from the safety of the alley, located almost directly across the street from the hotel restaurant, figurin' he couldn't miss at that range. He liked usin' the big Henry rifle because it held thirteen rounds and could put down ah man at ah distance further than he could see.

-

In another alley just a block up from where Clyde hid, Charlie Coots also stood at the corner of ah buildin', facin' the main street, and he too was lookin' in the direction of the hotel restaurant. A thirty-caliber Winchester lever action rifle rested against his shoulder; his finger itching ta pull the trigger. Millsap could have the ranger. He wanted the sheriff.

Between him and that ranger, they had cost him several thousand dollars, plus wipin' out their whole gang, ceptin' him and

Clyde. The time fer revenge was comin' up soon, and in ah few minutes there would be two less lawmen ta dog their trail.

Their plan was simple. Durin' all the excitement, Clyde would take down the ranger and he would take down the sheriff. When the two men were dead, they would hustle down the alleys, jump on their horses and be long gone before the town folks realized what had happened.

They still had ah bank job up in Fayetteville ta rob, which they hoped would make up for some of the money they'd lost taday.

-

When the townsfolk came filin' out of the restaurant, shoutin' and slappin' each other on the back, Clyde's adrenalin kicked in and he pulled the big rifle a little tighter against his shoulder. After wipin' sweat out of his eyes, he sighted down the barrel, waitin' fer the ranger ta walk inta his sights.

At last, the sheriff and the ranger came walkin' out onta the sidewalk. The sheriff was in good spirits and was enjoyin' all the attention the towns people were givin' him. The only one not celebratin' was Clay Brentwood. He would smile and nod his head when they congratulated him, tryin' not ta show his worry.

Clyde Millsap had not been among the dead, nor was he one of the men in the jail up the street. Clay was sure Clyde had been part of the bank robbery attempt, earlier today, so, where was he?

The man wouldn't just ride away; it wasn't in his nature.

As was his normal custom, Clay's eyes were trying to scan the area, but the sun was directly in his eyes and he couldn't see more than ten feet; not near far enough to see the other side of the street, and this made him nervous. He pulled the brim of his hat down enough so he could see the opposite side of the street.

Was it fate lookin' after him or was it the nail stickin' up outta one of the boards of the sidewalk that caused Clay ta trip?

Whichever it was, as he went forward, he put out his hands in front of him to try and catch his balance, and in doin' so, accidentally shoved the sheriff in the back, causin' him ta lunge forward.

As Clay fell forward, a cloud passed in front of the sun just enough for him to glimpse a metal reflection off a gun barrel in the alley across the street.

The impact of the 44-40 slug slammed into Clay's right leg and bore a hole all the way through, then imbedded itself in Clay's left thigh.

The impact of the big slug knocked him sideways and he hit the side of the hotel, then slid down to the sidewalk. Instinct alone caused Clay to fill his hand with his six shooter as his eyes searched for the shooter.

The last thing Clay remembered seein' was one of the men from town, runnin' in front of him, blockin' his view.

When Clay shoved the sheriff in the back, he was knocked forward and because he was movin' forward, he caught a 30-30-caliber bullet in his right arm instead of his chest.

At the sound of the two rifle shots, the men from Fort Smith, already keyed up, split up and ran in the direction of the two alleys, their guns drawn and shootin' at the unseen shooters.

When they reached the far ends of the alleys, they saw two men riding hard for the stand of trees in the distance.

Two men, Elmer Johnston and Henry Crawford, both, buffalo hunters, stepped forward and dropped to one knee. Each man carried a Sharps long rifle, model 1878. As one, they took their time and loaded a shell into their rifles. Then, in unison, they brought the rifles to their shoulders, nodded at each other and took aim.

By now, Clyde and Charlie were over three hundred yards away, and riding hard for the shelter of the trees.

Two shots that sounded like one, reverberated through the air and a moment later, Clyde Millsap and Charlie Coots were knocked from their horses and landed face down on the hard ground. Neither man would ever rob a bank or shoot at someone from ambush, again.

Brian Shipley, the barber, and Ralph Stevens, the dentist, headed for the livery barn to see about a wagon to retrieve the bodies of the two dead outlaws.

-

While this was goin' on, several of the townsmen had wasted no time getting' the two injured men over to the doctor's office.

Doctor Horace P. Collinsworth, the town's only doctor took one look at the two men covered with blood and had a flashback to a day, as a newly enlisted doctor in the Confederate Army. It had been the seventeenth of September eighteen-sixty-two. The battle of Antietam, or as some folks called it, the battle of Sharpsburg. It had been the first major battle during the Civil War that had taken place on union soil, and to this day, considered to be the bloodiest single day battle in American history, 22,717 dead, wounded or missing. Twenty-nine hours, he'd worked straight, trying to save lives to no avail. The blood and carnage had been almost more than he could bear.

Looking down at the two men covered with blood, he said a silent prayer, hoping to save the lives of these two men, but in his opinion, their chances were slim and none. He would do his best.

-

More than a hundred men and women stood around outside the doctor's office, waiting to hear the fate of the two lawmen.

"Glad they got them two miscreants," one of the men said.

Every person within earshot nodded his or her head in agreement.

After more than three hours of waitin', the doctor opened the door of his office and stepped out on the sidewalk. He was covered in blood and looked like he'd been through a war, himself.

Doctor Collinsworth looked at the faces staring back at him and took a deep breath. "When you brought the sheriff and the ranger to me, I have to be honest, I didn't give them much of a chance for survival. But, I'm a doctor and have sworn an oath to do all I can, no matter how bad they're injured."

Even the air had grown still as the people waited for the final outcome.

The doctor pointed toward his office and said, "Those two men in there are as tough as they come, and by the grace of God, I think they're gonna make it."

THE END

Thank you to all my readers. Your reviews and requests for more Clay Brentwood books is an inspiration to me. I'll keep writing them as long as you keep requesting them…

MEET THE AUTHOR

JARED McVAY is a four-time award-winning author. He writes several genres, including - westerns, fantasy, action/adventure, and children's books. Before becoming an author, he was a professional actor on stage, in movies and on television. As a young man he was a cowboy, a rodeo clown, a lumberjack, a power lineman, a world-class sailor and spent his military time with the Navy Sea Bees where he learned his electrical trade. When not writing you can find him fishing somewhere or traveling around and just enjoying life with his girlfriend, Jerri.

THANK YOU
FOR READING!

If you enjoyed this book, we would appreciate your customer review on your book seller's website or on Goodreads.

Also, we would like for you to know that you can find more great books like this one at

www.SixGunBooks.com

 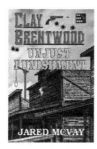 

Stories so real you can smell the gunsmoke.™

Made in the USA
Columbia, SC
05 January 2019